INDENTURED SCHOLARS:
The Inner City Scandal

by W. Ivan Wright

INDENTURED
SCHOLARS
the inner city scandal

Published by Able Journey Press
P.O. Box 5517
Trenton, New Jersey 08638-9998
(877) 650-3610
www.ablejourneypress.com
Book Design by Deesignz Web & Graphics Studio

Library of Congress Cataloging-in-Publication Data

Wright, W. Ivan
Indentured Scholars – The Inner City Scandal/ by W. Ivan Wright.
p. cm

ISBN: 9781934249475

2008900358

10 9 8 7 6 5 4 3 2 1

ABLE JOURNEY

DEDICATION

These pages are dedicated to the many silent heroes who fully understood that the road to advancement was illuminated by the liberating light of increased knowledge.

We honor their memory and untold sacrifices not by speeches or candles, but by pressing boldly forward on our respective journeys.

PROLOGUE

"There he is over there, don't lose em!"

Caleb Salisbury was still trying to catch his breath when he spotted the determined Negro zigzagging toward the wooden shanty homes that represented the distressed lower class of nineteenth century Philadelphia. Caleb, half-drunk, gestured to his fellow pursuers: a growing mob that was hot in pursuit of the dogged Negro. Caleb was not even sure of the man's crime. He was only aware that it had been a long, boring week and any sport was fair game to him. He had missed the big fight—he wouldn't miss the hunt.

The focus of Caleb's attention was Thaddeus Sanford, a 36-year-old black man whose only crime was protecting his family. The quiet and unassuming Thaddeus lived with his wife and three children in one of the colored areas of Philadelphia. Earlier that evening a nasty fight had broken out in the market area that served the disadvantaged of all races. The real purpose of the market was the activity that took place in the back: gambling.

When the police arrived at the fight scene, the crowd didn't disperse but instead chose to hang around to observe the unscheduled entertainment. It did not take long for the gathering to push upon one another. Exasperated, the officers muscled back, demonstrating their superiority in the sweltering stand-off. Loud shouts were soon followed by fisticuffs that were not initially directed at the officers, but nevertheless, resulted in an all-out donnybrook. The outnumbered officers, hoping to take control of the situation, resorted to the use of makeshift billy clubs. A few of the more drunken men in the crowd took exception to the disparity in weaponry and grabbed pick-ax handles from a nearby barrel.

Thaddeus, a wharf-loader by day, worked in the evening at the produce market cleaning up the splintered, moldy crates and preparing the orders for morning deliveries. His eleven-year-old son Daniel helped him at times. This evening Daniel was patiently waiting for his father to finish up so they could hurry home for supper. Taking note of the outside commotion, a socially seasoned Thaddeus chose to leave his work unfinished and hurry home with his son. With an angry crowd and angered policemen lurking, Thaddeus took a less traveled route away from the teeming mob.

As they set out, Daniel realized that he had left his favorite wood-carving knife near the cabbage bin. Before his father could stop him, he ran back inside to retrieve it. By the time he had returned, fists and clubs were flying and much of the crowd was running in all directions. Uncertain of whether or not to stay in the store or try to make it home, Thaddeus decided to lead his son through an area that was used as an unofficial refuse. In a dead run, they turned a corner and directly encountered the large frame of a cursing and bleeding policeman who had earlier been struck by a flailing pick-ax. The inflamed officer shoved Thaddeus into a garbage heap then turned to see who had grabbed his arm. As with all children of color, Daniel had been repeatedly instructed by his father to never touch a white man, let alone an officer: he was acting on reflex, trying to protect his father.

The policeman wasted no time in bringing up his club to strike the young boy. Daniel quickly crumpled to the ground anticipating the blow. Wide-eyed, he watched the backswing of the wooden baton as the officer prepared to deliver a more satisfying blow when his father's huge fist found the officer's jaw with a crippling force. The beer-bellied policeman fell back, striking his head on the end of an upturned, rusted carriage frame. Thaddeus was frightened.

He reached for his son and heard more footsteps, realizing that he would have to quickly get himself and Daniel away from the area. Half-carrying, half-dragging Daniel, Thaddeus hurried back toward the store. He was still able to hear the angry voices of the uniformed pursuers. Thaddeus's eyes darted around the area. He made a decision on impulse and shoved his whimpering son into the small opening of a grain box, warning him to remain silent and still until he returned for him. Thaddeus then sprinted in the direction of the main thoroughfare in hopes of both drawing the pursuit away from Daniel and blending in with the crowd. To his dismay, the crowed had waned. Thaddeus found himself almost alone as he sped toward a wooded area that he believed might offer him refuge.

He quietly waited for almost two numbing hours, hidden between two decaying felled trees, before he emerged from his place of hiding. Thaddeus could remain there no longer as thoughts of his dear son compelled him to return to the market area.

Daniel listened as the sounds of the street grew dim. The scurrying of local rats let him know that the area was essentially calm. He carefully used the obscured pathways, safely making his way home to his frantic mother.

Thaddeus felt the tension choking the air as the angry sounds of men polluted the night. What he did not know was that the policeman he had struck was now dead. It was Thaddeus that had been previously seen by the officers. It was Thaddeus that was the sole focus of the hunt. The initial battle in the market area was now ancient history. Both policemen, and those who had struggled against them in the early evening, were now unspoken allies in a primal quest to satisfy common hate.

Thaddeus tried to stay low, but his exhaustion made it difficult. He came upon the open porch of a house that sat by itself, hugging the tree line. He noted an elderly man, watching, swaying smoothly in an old, oversized rocker that creaked with each movement. Thaddeus dared to hope that perhaps this was a sympathetic soul who might offer him sanctuary; however, as he drew closer, he could tell that the smile on the old man's face was not one of compassion but of patient, dark malice.

Thaddeus quickly continued on, somewhat confused why such a foreboding face would not summon the malevolent mob to its prize. He kept moving, glancing back only to see an empty porch. Even while running for his life, Thaddeus realized that not only was the man gone, but the porch was also without the rocker.

Someone on horseback in the distance spotted Thaddeus. He once again found himself in bursting flight for his life. Twisting and turning through the dirt-graveled streets, he thought that he had again separated himself from capture until he heard the outcry of someone pointing him out. There ceased to be any distinction between the law and the citizenry as the sound of footsteps grew and shots rang out. A lonely bullet claimed a fiery home in Thaddeus' side. He ran on for a few steps then fell in a heap near a stack of cobblestones.

"Well, boy, I do believe that your luck has done run out," hollered one of the policemen.

"Whudya think, we was just gonna let you get away with killin' a white man?" said Caleb, his hairy chest heaving from sweet anticipation.

"I didn't kill nobody," Thaddeus's voice cracked. "Just protecting my family, protecting my boy."

"Well, Officer Boatwright is now dead. He ain't coming back; it was you we seen."

Thaddeus had now lost a lot of blood and was barely able to see the presiding membership of Philadelphia's unofficial nocturnal court. He realized that he would never again set eyes on family or home. His only solace was the fact that no one made any mention of looking for his beloved Daniel. His glazed eyes slowly rolled back as his last words were whispered for only the heavens to hear, "Just wanted to protect my family—will always protect my family. Daniel, you'se always be's safe."

The mob was disappointed that death had made its claim so quickly. They tossed the lifeless body of their victim in the back of a wood cart, then dumped it on a dusty roadway. Friends of the Sanford family silently retrieved his body and sorrowfully presented it to the new widow. The strong, proud man who had dared to entertain hopes of seeing his children grow old and more prosperous than he was committed to decay in the stony, unfriendly earth of Philadelphia's colored cemetery.

CHAPTER ONE

"What do you *mean* I can't see my child until Christmas? It's August right now! Just what is wrong with you people? You just can't be coming into someone's house and snatch away their child. You just can't, and that's that!" Mrs. Nora Sanford spoke, jawbones throbbing. She was a widow of three years who had once dreamed of a humble but comfortable future with her now-deceased husband, Malcolm Sanford.

The voice that responded was one of familiar patience. Its tone was honed from having often been the recipient of an angry retort.

"Now, Mrs. Sanford." George Kinder saw a cockroach but pretended he hadn't.

"Don't you 'Mrs. Sanford' me." She sat her cup on the coffee table.

"My sincere apologies, Mrs. Sanford, no offense meant. But you know that we have been through this before, and in fact, you stated that you really wanted this: for yourself and more importantly, for LeDain."

"I know, I know… but not until Christmas? That's much too long. I love my baby too much to be away from him for so long."

George Kinder, the administrative secretary of New Passage Academy, gave a small sigh and leaned back on a sofa that had seen better days. He shifted his back to find a position within the bumps that would result in the minimum of discomfort. Kinder applauded himself for not giving any acknowledgement of the occasional multi-legged tenants that scurried across the faded, spackled walls. The ultimate test was always the manner in which he would skillfully deflect the offer of a beverage or snack. Disrespect was never his intention, so for each visit he rehearsed a response during the car ride over.

1

The refrigerator in the small kitchen in the next room emitted a groaning hum that at times, seemed to mimic someone getting ready to speak. He could have sworn that he once heard the refrigerator emit a grating laugh. Mr. Kinder always noted that there were never any crusted dishes piled in the sink, nor were there any scattered food items on the table that would imply an indifference to home sanitation. He had long since recognized that housekeeping skills knew no specific demographic. Clearly Mrs. Sanford possessed a basic sense of decency and respect for herself.

"Please, Mrs. Sanford, I do not believe that anyone could ever love your son even half as much as you, but is it not that very love that guided you to the decision to make sure that your son would have more opportunities for the betterment of his life?" Mr. Kinder gave her time to respond as he quietly pondered the safety of his Lexus. This neighborhood was not ideal.

"Yes, I know, Mr. Kinder; you have been patient with your explanation. It's just that it's one thing to hear it and another thing to hear it out loud. You know what I'm saying? I mean, you have to admit that this is a whole lot to take in. Maybe we'd just better leave things be. We all just might be fine here."

"No offense meant, Mrs. Sanford. Perhaps you should again hear yourself out loud. Even if I never showed up at your door, do you really believe that your children have the best possibilities—*here?*" He gestured to the rundown house.

Nora put her head in her hands. Too many issues and questions fought to gain first row seating in her thoughts. She finally responded: "But I don't know anything about the school, about you. You haven't shown me any brochures or anything."

"No, I haven't. There are no brochures, and you won't find any information regarding the school on any website. We don't even have a parents' newsletter. You see, Mrs. Sanford, the only way that we have achieved such a phenomenal success in producing outstanding students is by being…well, invisible." She gave a puzzled look.

"Let me explain." He leaned forward. "The reason I'm here is because our school has tracked your boy's test records. We then did some more of our usual, let's say, homework, and here we are. What I can offer you here tonight will only be for tonight. If you decline, and you have every right to do so, you will not be able to find me or hear from me again." He paused for effect. "But yes, certainly you should know where your child is going. To that end, our school would cover your travel arrangements so you could see for yourself just what we have in store for your son's future."

"This really doesn't make sense to me. How can you be so secretive and still have parents visit their children? Someone would have found out by now."

"Oh, once you get there, you'll see how we've been able to maintain our secrecy. It's really very interesting. I would love to be able to show you and—"

"Whoa, wait a minute! I haven't agreed to anything, Mr. Kinder. I know that you think I'm probably being paranoid and all, but sometimes, depending on where you live, paranoia is necessary for survival. I'm just a single mom in the hood. I know that I ain't knowing things that people like you be knowing, but I do know that I love my son, and I'm really in no hurry to give him up." She crossed her arms, subconsciously demonstrating her resolve in the matter. "Actually this all is sounding kind of spooky," she added. "And I don't even think that LeDain would want to be bothered and all."

Mr. Kinder put up his hand and gave a knowing smile. "It's okay, Mrs. Sanford. I don't mean to sound so… so mysterious. Forgive me please. All I ask of you is to give me ten more minutes of your time and I'll be gone."

"Well, I don't know."

"I'm not speaking for me, but for Mr. Sanford."

"Who… Mr. Sanford? I told you my husband is dead." Her brows raised.

"I am speaking of Mr. LeDain Sanford," Mr. Kinder's tone changed. "We at New Passage Academy like to immediately give the students a sense of the respect and dignity, which is their social expectation." Nora cast a gaze on the ceiling, giving away the fact that she was fully envisioning a young man who would be habitually and respectfully addressed as Mr. Sanford—her son.

"Well, ten minutes isn't too long to give, I guess."

"Thank you, Ms. Sanford, please let me explain. I'm aware that you have both of your boys living here with you."

"Yes, that's right. I don't know where my eldest is right now. I try to be firm with Jared, but he's getting to have a mind of his own. He's a good boy; he's still sweet, it's just that..." He could see that she was trying to catch her thoughts as well as her breath. He glanced away to allow her personal space. "It's just that he's becoming more by himself and not coming home when I tell him to and all. I know that he's getting caught up more and more in this street mess." She wiped her wet eyes—a mother's love met head-on with life's frustrations.

"Actually, Mrs. Sanford, I kind of already knew what Jared was doing. That's really what I'm getting at. You see, although I really don't know you or your oldest son, I believe that he most certainly is a good boy who was taught well. There was just more time for him to pick up the negative than your busy time allowed for positive. Mrs. Sanford, I know that your day is mostly spent trying to keep the family warm, fed, and with decent clothes on their backs. It's a struggle enough for two people, let alone a single mother."

"I wasn't always single. My husband, my husband Malcolm, was killed on the job a few years back. The foreman on his job kinda forgot to tell the repair people that Malcolm was still working in the cardboard compactor when someone turned it back on. Oh, they heard him right away but by the time someone hit the kill switch, it was too late." For a moment she silently stared at the wall. "Yeah, that's a real funny name for that type of button—a *kill* switch."

Mr. Kinder gave her a few moments before he continued his quiet but passionate argument regarding the academy.

"You are making many sacrifices for your sons so tell me, what might you sacrifice for the opportunity for LeDain to be academically prepared and able to welcome adulthood as a financially successful man?" Mr. Kinder leaned forward to better capture her gaze. "I guess another question might be: just where do you see Jared as an adult? I am not wishing anything bad on him, I'm not. We all know that many have succeeded even when they've faced odds such as Jared's. They, too, succeeded against all odds."

As if on cue, the unmistakable sound of distant gunfire made its way into the living room. It would be another fifteen minutes before police sirens were heard. Mr. Kinder saw Mrs. Sanford flinch. He first thought it was from the urge to lie on the floor, to be beneath window level. He quickly realized that it was her mental search for her son that gave her skin frozen tremors. He pondered the gross inequality of an American Mother's Day. Just having children gives all concerned parents a protective pause. Worries include marginal grades, unknown friends, or the propensity to try something, just once. Why should some mothers have to experience the heartache of a knock on the door with a municipal official asking questions regarding the clothes that their child might have worn? How many places are there for one's heart to leap when asked if their child has any distinguishable features? Mr. Kinder wet his lips.

"The magic question, of course, is do we like the odds? Truly, just what are the chances, his chances? What if the odds against your LeDain were somehow changed from being monumentally against him into magnificently for him? That's why I'm here, Mrs. Sanford, to realign the odds...with your permission, of course."

Nora gave no response but her body language revealed the turmoil that was playing in her head. She loved LeDain. She loved both her sons and was joyful when she could wrap her arms around them as night became morning. It was unfair that her love had to be tried in such a way. While part of her wished that Mr. Kinder had never found out about her or LeDain, the other part understood that her prayers were merely being addressed. How often had she implored God to make things better for her family? But why would God answer in such a cruel way? If only her husband were still alive. But then again, *Malcolm, did you send this man my way?*

"I'm sorry, what were you saying? Didn't get the last part of what you were..." She immediately tensed as sounds came from the front stoop. *Was it Jared, or was it someone regarding him?* She relaxed slightly as she realized that it was only one of the neighborhood kids, a six-year-old still free to roam the darkened streets. Kinder watched her glances and her body movements. He understood the language of parenting enough to know that Mrs. Sanford had only been given a brief reprieve. She would have to again endure all her motherly emotions with the next sound at her door.

"It's quite all right, ma'am, I know that it's been a long day for you. Allow me to be a bit clearer: some years back, a few well-meaning philanthropists gave a major financial endorsement toward the creation of a school that would provide a premium education to disadvantaged children of color. This school has been around for almost thirty years. Unfortunately, increased technology has probably caught up with us, and secrecy may be at an end. Nevertheless, we will maintain the course of our mission: to do our part in attempting to realign some of the inevitable negative residuals of social segregation." He studied her eyes. "Mrs. Sanford, we absolutely know that children, all children, are very capable of the highest learning. We are not trying to prove that, no need to. What we do strive to do is to perform our part in touching just a few lives. Grant it, the need for such a school has decreased as other academic institutions have discovered their suppressed sense of ethics. But still, the need persists. Money is not an issue with our academy. Our educational staff has the credentials to teach at any major institution of higher learning, but to tell you the truth, we just pay better—much better." Kinder was really thirsty. He just couldn't get past the cockroaches.

"Our students not only receive a superbly premier education, but they are also vigorously instructed in life skills that will further equip them for success. Understand that our measure of success includes the desire for the graduate to better their environment. It is up to them to define their respective communities."

Ten minutes had long passed, but Mrs. Sanford was mesmerized by the school even though a part of her understood that it was out of her reach. Mr. Kinder was on it.

"Now, Mrs. Sanford, I know what you're probably thinking right now. I'm not here to sell you anything. What I am doing is, hopefully, being clear on the profound opportunity that simply awaits your decision. The question is, is LeDain deserving of such a place? Do you believe that such a school would, in ten years or so, have your child positioned to be a leader in business or government? I again pose the question: is LeDain worthy of at least that consideration?"

An emotionally drained Mrs. Sanford leaned back on the sofa and gave an almost inaudible, "Yes. Yes, he is. But how, where does such a place exists? I mean, do we talk of scholarships, grants and loans? It all sounds real good, Mr. Kinder, but I couldn't begin to pay even a little of what a place like that probably cost. Damn, it does sound like quite a school."

"Mrs. Sanford, it is quite a school; we are prepared to accept LeDain into our school at exactly no cost to you whatsoever—today, or in the future."

"Okay, now you're really making no sense," said Mrs. Sanford as her face exhibited a clear Negro-please glare. "Top education, the best staff, and you don't even want me to stand at the supermarket with a donation basket? It's kinda still not making a lot of sense to me, Mr. Kinder. I love my son but he's not exactly busting any exams wide open."

"It's all right, no one has to be busting any exams right now. We like to think of a child as a bank. A bank that perhaps is sitting on the corner with $50 million or so, a full vault. However, most people are only asking to withdraw small amounts: you know, just needing a thousand dollars here or perhaps a fifteen-thousand dollar loan there. No one comes in and asks for $50 million. Doesn't mean that it's not there, but it just never is requested. Might as well call the bank a dollar store, as that's all that's demanded of it. Sometimes our children are never asked to give anything more than what someone or some test needs. People learn to expect small dollars from our children, and soon, that's all our children believe that they have." She hung on to his words. "Your son is real, Mrs. Sanford, and full of potential. We at the New Passage Academy will hold up the mirror so LeDain can take a long peek and see all that he is worth, see all the riches that are stacked in his mind as well as in his spirit."

Nora was almost crying. A part of her gave way, permitting her own spirit to think that her child could be a student in such a school. She blinked the tears loose.

"Yes. Yes, I would love for my LeDain to attend the school. What do I need to sign? What do I need to do?" Kinder straightened his tie as he paused, capturing her puffing eyes.

"This is the hard part. As I've said before: what you have to do is release your child to us. We aren't taking him from you; we are merely doing those things that will allow your son to absolutely focus on his future." He crossed his legs. The sofa was beginning to take its toll on his lower back. "Understand this: You will only be permitted to see him three times a year. In other words, Mrs. Sanford, your child will become a permanent resident of New Passage Academy." She bowed her head and repeatedly poked her forehead with stiffened fingers. She was determined to keep the insanity demons at bay. Her head remained bowed, eyes still closed as she slowly rocked and spoke to Mr. Kinder.

"Why would you build my hopes up like this? It sounded so good that I almost forgot about that part." Mr. Kinder sat up to regain a more formal posture.

"We really do understand that this is not an easy decision. What loving parent would want to give up her child? Of course we understand," he said, worrying about his Lexus again. "There's something else that we understand. Children living in certain neighborhoods, in certain areas, face an overwhelming number of problems that can steer them away from having a meaningful life." He did not bring up the name of her eldest son, Jared. It wasn't necessary: Kinder could see Jared's name in her eyes.

"Can we agree that all the love that you can muster still can't change the fact that each day takes Jared closer and closer to a life that is totally against your values and vision?" It was as if he was reading her mind. "Even with the best of intentions and motherly love, sooner or later Jared might join up with the predators just to save his own life? If I walk out of the door empty-handed, will LeDain's tomorrows be an echo of his brother's?" Mr. Kinder took a chance and lightly touched her hand. "Do we allow LeDain a new door of shining possibilities?"

The noise of an upstairs television grew louder as the familiar sounds of someone turning stations came into the room. As with most commercials, the sound was set higher than the scheduled program, ensuring one's attention regarding a new, revolutionary diet plan. Both adults paused as they heard LeDain settle in on a cartoon show.

"Ooh, Scooby Doo," said Mr. Kinder, grinning. "My favorite."

Nora gave him a puzzled look. She assumed him to be one of those 'money-market' program watchers. Mr. Kinder held his impish grin, understanding her thoughts. "Hey, we're not out to make soulless robots, I'd eat LeDain up in PlayStation." Her head now angled farther to the right, giving this man in the expensive suit another look. "Oh, yes, I am good, thank you very much. We have PlayStation; we just understand that it's not called, 'Play-*all*-the-time-Station'." She leaned back and laughed. Mr. Kinder's grin turned into a smile. He knew that the New Passage Academy had gained a new student.

CHAPTER TWO

Chadric Pearson was leaning against his silver Mercedes S600. This was no afternoon for a love-my-Mercedes commercial. His arms were folded across his chest; his jaw was set, matching his stare. The object of his discomfort was the scrawny old man leaning next to him.

Fellyard Beedley had accosted Chadric as he exited the intricately adorned glass doors of his luxury high-rise building. Chadric had initially failed to recognize the slightly built man, but as soon as Fellyard's voice gave salutation, Chadric had frozen in his steps. No one else could possibly possess that same voice. His morning appointment was now forgotten: it was evident that Fellyard had a focused agenda and would not be put off. Boney fingers squeezed Chadric's right elbow, steering him toward the valet parking section of the high-rise's entrance.

"We have to work together to get rid of the problem, nephew," said Fellyard. "I know that you understand this and will be with me on this. You won't let me down, will you?" The old man's breath was hot and hollow. He stood close to Chadric, emphasizing his point.

"Hell, there are plenty of other good-looking chicks out there for you to marry. We can't let her expose my school. I'm just beginning to get a better foothold regarding the quality of the faculty, but I need more time to move some others out of the way. Yes, it's going to happen, can't fail again," he said.

"I don't understand," said Chadric. "I thought that the faculty and other such matters were in the hands of the national board. It almost sounds as if there's been a change in leadership."

"And why not?" Fellyard's gaze was dead serious. "Change is good. You know that we can't operate under the same

10

umbrella and techniques of days gone by. You know the saying: a new world order."

"So why are you bothering me, what does my love life have to do with the school?" Chadric looked at Fellyard. "What do you mean by 'getting rid' of the problem?"

A stranger sat on the concrete step of a closed tax office wearing a loosely fitting army camouflage jacket and slowly munching on an apple. The stranger fully understood the irony of such a jacket in the city: to wear military camouflage in this urban environment was an invitation to actually stand out. Still, the man also understood the awesome power of invisibility belonging to those who frequented the streets. It was the battle of competing social perceptions. Which truth wielded the greater sovereignty? Mostly it was society's apathy that ruled supreme. The propensity for military camouflage to stand out was usually defeated by the invisibility of those without a permanent address. Today, the stranger sat on a step surveying the area where the two men were stood against a silver Mercedes.

Chadric turned to give a long look at Fellyard, capturing his eyes.

"What do you mean by 'getting rid' of the problem?"

Fellyard echoed the stare, seeking to identify the rigidity of Chadric's resolve. "Calm down lover boy." Fellyard's vacant yet focused stare held Chadric's eyes. He chose his words carefully: aiming to minimize panic and also confirm an avenue of manipulation. "It is important that we speak again. I remember you as one of the strong ones—one of the *special* ones. I'm sorry that you had to make other plans. How many years ago was it?"

"Are we finished here?" Chadric counted to five in his head. "Let me restate that: we *are* finished here. You're not in everyone's head."

"Don't let me hold you up, I know that you're a busy man. We can talk later. You never know where I'm bound to show up. I do get around, you know? Good day, nephew."

It appeared to the camouflage-wearing stranger that the young man was not very pleased with the encounter. Distance precluded the ability to listen in, but the very presence of the older man appeared to cause the younger man an almost physical discomfort. The stranger leaned partially to the side, resting his head on the railing of the steps. His eyes were glued to the private meeting. The stranger's mental library informed him that he had seen the senior member of the distant meeting before, but where? What bothered the stranger more than anything was the fact that he had initially wanted to get a closer look at the younger man. The sudden appearance of the older man had thrown everything off. *Dammit, where have I seen the old coot before?* For a moment he believed that perhaps it was a memory born in his midnight hours; a visitor to the tortured dreams founded in restless sleep.

The stranger again focused his gaze on the younger man as he reached into one of his many pockets to finger the handle of his .38 revolver. He quickly released the handle and drew his jacket closer together as he received a look from an officer in a passing police car. He took one last look at the two men and turned down the street, muttering a silent expletive in the direction of the police car.

Cops always thinking that they know something. I got a home, I got an address. People always think that they know. Just prefer the solitude of the street, that's all. Sometimes being at home by yourself can be... so loud.

CHAPTER THREE

A cloudless sky sent warmed ultraviolet daggers toward the mundane, toward crinkled eyes. Even still, the majestic natural ceiling was all too wonderful a sight to leave unobserved. The air held a subtle sweetness, opening doors to childhood memories of playing in the park and being allowed to yell without consequence or judgment. With another deep breath, one could almost see the playmates of years gone by, see the small ears muted to the voices of alien adults but sharply attuned to the melody of a rusty-rimmed ice cream truck that was holding court blocks away. Birds glided lazily. Even insects agreed to give the gangly humans distance on this afternoon. It was a made-to-order afternoon for a romantic wedding in the park.

Synthia Godbold stood with her arms draped around her stoic-faced father as the first chords of the Bridal March lifted into the August air. Silky breezes gave a slight lift to her lovely veil, granting her silhouette a regal presentation.

Ben Campbell was actually Synthia's stepfather. It had never mattered. He leaned forward to whisper into his daughter's ear but he understood that his daughter's eyes were on her fiancé. For this brief moment, Dad had her ear. Synthia made eye contact and gave her father a gentle squeeze: no words were needed.

Chadric stood proudly between Reverend Sydney and Ted, his best man. Chadric's dark complexion was in stark contrast with the fairness of Reverend Sydney and Ted. Chadric's features would never be confused with those of Denzel or Boris Kodjoe, yet his countenance somehow summoned a strong sexual attraction. Chadric's eyes were deep-set, giving him an unusual allure. When entering a room, his posture and bearing commanded respect; his voice was firm, always in control and never pretentious.

Early on in their relationship, when Synthia had shown Chadric's picture to a few ladies at her workplace, someone had questioned her choice of such a plain and rugged mate. The question came from Tammy, one of the network staff who believed that only a fair-headed Adonis should share the arms of such a fly public figure. After meeting Chadric at a news station function, Tammy had quickly changed her mind, as well as her game plan. Her concern for Synthia became evident when she attempted to test Chadric's allegiance to Synthia by making every effort to gain eye contact and touch him. With discipline and charm, Chadric let Tammy know that she was wasting her time. He reminded Tammy of the fact that her status as a friend of Synthia was indeed in jeopardy.

"Stunning, isn't she?" said Reverend Sydney, bringing Chadric back to the present.

"More than you'll ever know, Reverend." Chadric couldn't keep from smiling.

"As it should be." The reverend winked.

Synthia and her father made the traditional flowered sojourn down the aisle. Each step took her closer toward her beloved. She exchanged glances with close friends and family as they stood with appreciative smiles. Synthia offered one last look to her father as the reverend ended his query of "Who gives this woman?" Perhaps her father didn't hear it or couldn't hear it. She squeezed his hand. He reluctantly released his grip and made the painful steps to his awaiting seat.

Leena Gaston, Synthia's cousin, was the matron of honor. Next to her stood Taylea Snead, Synthia's hairstylist. Forever talkative and animated, even Taylea's smile was loud. Her husband sat quietly in the rear of the outdoor sanctuary, vainly attempting to mentally will Taylea into calmness.

When the bride and groom had finished with their respective pledging of sacred vows, all eyes turned to Keenan, Taylea's nephew. He was poised to render a song. One could almost read the thought-balloons floating in the air. Most seasoned wedding-goers understood that the wedding soloist was the result of a coin toss. Most understood that all too often it was decided by family association and not always skill. Sometimes the song flowed; many times it was an exercise in courteous audience restraint. Many hearts froze; frontal teeth almost drew blood as some clamped down on their bottom lips. All had recognized the familiar chords of Luther Vandross's *Here and Now* as it rose from a Yamaha keyboard. *Oh no, not Luther! Please, don't mess up Luther!* The reverend crossed his fingers. Some heads lowered and went down in silent prayer; even the nonbelievers joined in.

God is alive. Heads rose as Keenan's voice proved to be talented and soulful. By the time he had finished, some had even forgotten the traditional decorum of the wedding ceremony and started to stand in ovation. Synthia blew the embarrassed Keenan a kiss as he made his way to his seat.

Reverend Sydney brought the ceremony to a close and uttered the familiar order which granted the gathering permission to salute the bride. Leena performed her traditional task; Synthia's veil was lifted, and she received her first kiss as Mrs. Pearson. The obligatory oohs and ahhs sang out from among the guests as the husband and wife gave a slightly prolonged version of the typically short salute. Hands that once clasped the firm security of her father's arms now encircled the mystery of her new husband's. The newlyweds' sparkling eyes now matched the dancing sky. The couple strolled toward the rose-adorned archway.

CHAPTER **FOUR**

The wedding party and all the invited guests were assembled in the reception area of a private park. Lively chatter and mellow music met in wondrous concert.

"Hey girl, you did it," Taylea said, hugging Synthia. "Your hair looks wonderful!" She then surprised everyone watching by placing a big, wet one on the laughing lips of Chadric. Taylea took a quick look at Synthia. "Don't worry, honey, that will be last time," Taylea said, laughing as Synthia's forced frown promptly eased into a laugh.

Taylea stood back and looked Synthia over. "Girl you look simply beautiful, simply beautiful. Doesn't she, Chadric?" Chadric started to answer but decided against it: no answer was expected. "And your hair, I just love it! Who did it? Oh, me, that's right, me. I almost forgot!" Taylea leaned forward and spoke to Synthia. "I am so happy for you and Chadric. Take care of each other. I just love you, you hear?"

Roland Snead, Taylea's husband, stood slightly behind her as she spoke with Synthia and Chadric. Roland was familiar with "girlfriend time," so he instead leaned toward Chadric and congratulated him with a bear hug. Chadric had met Roland once before, so he was not totally taken aback by the smothering clasp of the muscled man.

"Careful Roland, don't break him," said Taylea. "Synthia needs a fully working man tonight." Chadric grinned while Roland blushed and backed away.

"Taylea," said Synthia, "you never change."

"Naw, won't happen." Taylea tugged Roland's sleeve. "I'd better let you mingle with the other guests. Roland, what do you think?"

"You're right, baby. What was I thinking, holding up the bride and groom like this?" Synthia laughed. "Why, I do believe that Roland got one in on you, Taylea." Synthia laced her fingers with Chadric's. "Yeah, I guess he did, didn't he? Might have to give him a spanking for that later on. Daddy been bad." Synthia gave her friend a playful push. "Goodbye, Taylea."

"See you at the wedding cake," said Taylea. "Come on, Roland, the band sounds pretty good. Let's go see if they know any Kool and the Gang. Did I ever tell you about the time that I was almost lead singer for Rose Royce?" Roland rolled his eyes and took his wife's hand as she began her ever-changing story.

Amidst the gaiety, seated near an obliging tree, was the wizened form of an old man. He had positioned himself to be out of the line of sight of the guests. Even for those who might easily glance in his direction, he still remained obscured within the tree's disconcerting shadows. He spoke to no one and even waved away a guest who had ventured his way to initiate courteous conversation.

"Well, I guess you did it, Mr. Pearson," he said to himself. "You fell into the marriage trap—now only trouble awaits you." He finally stood up and walked toward a footpath. He stole one last glance at the new couple. "You never listen, nephew, you never listen."

Near the front entrance of the park another solitary figure stood observing the wedding festivities. He was a middle-aged man of stout stature with salt-speckled hair. His clothing was simple, yet obviously clean. He had, however, skipped the ironing portion of the laundry exercise. He noticed the departure of the older man who had sat alone under the tree. In his hand, he clutched a small photograph, glancing at it now and then as if to confirm its match to his current object of attention. Shifting his weight from one foot to the other, he appeared to be ill at ease with his own body. A closer inspection revealed the presence of a well-nicked cane. Perhaps the cane had once proudly bore the shining gleam of treated wood. The best it could do now was offer a faded resemblance to a stalk of long-discarded sugar cane.

Both man and cane held to each other like old friends declaring their right to be.

Synthia and Chadric's wedding was an invitation-only affair, and because of her moderate celebrity status, a security detail had been employed. One of the security officers took notice of the silent man but quickly determined him to be neither a physical threat, nor a potential wedding crasher. The officer had no idea of the pistol that was secreted in the man's trouser pocket.

He stood for a while longer, almost frozen. He observed the first dance of the bride and groom. His eyes squinted as he sought to better focus on the faces of the distant couple. His face remained without expression as the couple kissed. Determining that he had seen enough, and that the maladies of the body were summoning his full attention, he took a firmer grip on the handle of his walking partner and ambled toward the distant parking lot.

CHAPTER FIVE

Synthia and Chadric's honeymoon week was a wonderful storybook blur. The mounting stress and anxiety that attached itself to their wedding plans had, like a circus clown's balloon, been gleefully released into the air. In its place resided the hypnotic peace of lover's Soma. The clinging newlyweds had nibbled, danced, and explored. A couple of days later, they had even checked out the Hawaiian island.

The only part of the honeymoon that troubled Synthia was an incident in the hotel lobby. On the fifth day of their vacation, Chadric had left the room to make a purchase at the hotel gift shop. Synthia was still in the shower when Chadric yelled that he would be back in fifteen minutes. After drying and changing into fresh clothes, she decided to go down to the gift shop and make some purchases of her own. She was not overly concerned when she did not see Chadric there. Perhaps he had decided to step out of the hotel to inhale a breeze or two of the island's wonderful air. *Guess I should slow down a bit. Gonna make my man lose all of his oxygen trying to take care of sista girl. Well, can't live forever.* She grinned.

Bag in hand, Synthia left the shop and was making her way to the elevator when she spotted Chadric seated in the far corner of the lobby. He was not alone but was speaking to an older gentleman. *That's nice,* she thought, *Chadric has made a new friend.* As she held her gaze, she observed that the manner in which they were seated was not the casual posture of vacationing tourists. Both men leaned toward the other in a way that implied clandestine whisperings. The elevator door opened, but for some reason she could not move forward. Something was not quite right. Although the lobby of the Hawaiian hotel was brightly illuminated, they appeared to be conversing almost within shadows. A coldness crept along her limbs. She realized that she had seen this old man before, but where? The way he sat stirred something in her memory. She swore out loud. *Too many Mai Tais, young lady,* she said to herself. The bell rang, signaling the arrival of the elevator. She stepped forward but turned one last time to glance at the seated men. They were gone.

"Now someone has to tell me just how the existence of a private academy can be held from the public for so long? It's not making any sense to me," said Philadelphia's Mayor, Carlton Fountain, in a conference room at City Hall. The effects of the long day were evident throughout the room. The private conference room was filled with late afternoon attendees who had been hastily called together for a crisis meeting.

"Come on, Al. You're supposed to be the brains of this room," said Mayor Fountain. "Give us something."

"Not much to give, Mr. Mayor. I'm just as in the dark as all of us sitting here. This information is also new to me. I must admit, however, it is very intriguing."

"Well, intriguing or not, the problem is smack bang in front of our faces." The mayor's eyes darted around the room. "Let me state this very clearly: I for one am totally against this so-called prestigious institution. Anything that is held in secret will yield little that is good. All we have to do is look out of the window and see the people out there in protest at this private academy. Those folks are protesting about something that has essentially snuck up on us. That is totally unacceptable."

Al Connell was a senior member of the assembled mind trust. Throughout the years, he had worn many hats in the political game and was always a survivor. He currently served as deputy mayor, having stepped into the position almost two years ago following the murder of his predecessor. He served the city well. He continued to be the confidant of not only the mayor, but also of many well-heeled entities. The mayor gave his second-in-command a look of exasperation.

"Now you're telling me that we have a school that has been teaching young black students for almost thirty years, and no one in this room knows anything about it?"

"With all due respect, we know no more than you, Your Honor," someone said.

"All right, all right... duly noted," said Mayor Fountain. "So where do we go from here?"

"After all is said and done," said the deputy mayor, "Just what is the problem? Hasn't the school merely been trying to address the issues that we've all been fighting for the past three decades? Without success, I might add."

"Now we know that that's not the point," said Mayor Fountain. "The big issue, of course, is that parents, especially young mothers, are signing away their children. We just can't have that."

Councilman Donovan Utely yawned. He set down his metal-rimmed glasses and addressed the conference table. "Looking at the crime statistics as well as the statistics from our schools, haven't the students been signed away already? Should the crisis be a secret academy? Or should the actual crisis-hungry media blitz be directed toward the schools that are visible?"

"Come on," said the mayor. "You know we are not here to debate the pros and cons of such an academy. We know that this table has mixed opinions regarding this school, but we have to be very cautious in our response. Who else do we need in here? What's the use of having spin doctors if we can't get someone to put a spin on this thing?"

"It's not that we won't address it," said Deputy Mayor Connell. "It's just that I don't feel settled in myself for trying to expose a problem that by itself may soon fade away."

Someone spoke loudly from the rear. "I don't care what anyone at this table thinks, taking a child from its mother is wrong, just wrong. I don't care to put any spin on anything, and I'm insulted by anyone who thinks differently." Assemblywoman Florence Pendleton looked around the room and held her gaze on each person to ensure that there was no mistaking her resolve regarding the recruitment practices of New Passage Academy. Pendleton was a long-term representative of the Pennsylvania area. She held a lot of power. She also held the keys to many skeleton-lined closets and few dared to cross her. Even though the meeting was not strictly within her jurisdiction, this was one of those exceptional issues that crossed political borders.

"I don't think anyone is trying to slip anything under the rug here, Assemblywoman Pendleton," said Mayor Fountain. "All we're saying is, let's just move cautiously regarding this matter."

"As long as caution is not synonymous with remaining frozen or administratively impotent." Her tone was easy: "This is serious business. As a mother, I wouldn't want anyone to strong-arm me into giving up my child. Motherhood is a special and precious thing, and no one can take a mother's place—no one and no thing." She gave the mayor a long look then continued. "Now, you know that this has come to light because a young mother wasn't getting any satisfaction from her good friends at City Hall: go figure. Perhaps if someone had listened earlier, we wouldn't have a crowd outside now. Keep pissing on folks, they soon send it back your way." No one in the room said a word as Pendleton continued. "Now a mother is looking for her son. What do you think… that she's just going to stop looking because someone closes the door on her? That's why we're here: she started to yell to anyone who would listen— can you hear her now?"

"From a legal standpoint, is a crime being committed?" Councilman Utely repeatedly tapped an ink pen against a pad.

Assemblywoman Pendleton's voice grew louder: "I think we all understand that it's not just a matter of legal positioning. The problem speaks to the very fabric of society as it pertains to children and parents. No one can feel settled in their spirit with the image of a child being separated from his mother."

Al Connell, fearful of no one, yet always diplomatic, stood his ground and addressed the Assemblywoman. No one knew that the other reason for Al's freedom of speech was the fact that the late seventies had found the two political neophytes involved in a brief but steamy nonpolitical encounter.

"I believe that the accepted standards of our new society might be a bit different nowadays. We all agree that this world is an evolved beast. Once we take a deep breath, separation may not be such a bad thing. Some may say that many children are already separated form their mothers. Many children unfortunately grow up to be an antisocial element of society. Instead of innocent children, they are perceived as predators. I know it's not a warm statement; it's not a pretty picture."

"Yeah, I know what you're saying," said Councilman Utely. "We now have mothers and grandmothers, fathers and grandfathers who are barely out of childhood themselves. The problem is that even if they are technically adults because of their age, maturity never made the required transition. I think we would be surprised at just how many people don't take offense at an academy that requires parents to sign over their children."

"So, just what are you all saying?" Assemblywoman Pendleton looked at each person. "We just abandon all aspects of society as it pertains to parents and children? We just surrender? It's all okay now?"

"Not all believe that it is a matter of abandonment or surrender." Randice Newton offered up her opinion. Councilwoman Newton was a relatively new member of the City Council. She was smart, pretty, and took no *stuff* from anyone. Randice knew she looked good. She briefly boasted her appeal to be noticed, then it was time to move onto business.

Assemblywoman Pendleton turned and glared in her direction, annoyed at the verbal intrusion by the new upstart. She mentally filed away the name Randice Newton for future reference.

"Oh, so you don't think it's a matter of surrender? And as a woman you'll have no problem with someone snatching a child from your arms? You're telling me that it's a win-win scenario? It's all right that you can't see your child, Councilwoman Newton?"

Randice Newton held her ground: "This country is filled with people who hire nannies to watch over their children and there are no political meetings being called. Those same children finish their nanny phase and many are then sent away to some distant private school. No one has a problem with those children meeting up with mom and pops only during winter break, if then.

Don't forget, we come from a history where the elite would even pass off nursing their own baby to someone else."

"Well, thank you for that little lesson Harriet Tubman, but we're not discussing the elite. Let me remind you that we are speaking about those who have little financial voice and essentially no political leverage." Assemblywoman Pendleton was just about fed up with Newton.

"That's precisely why someone started the academy." Newton wasn't backing off.

Touché, thought the half-smiling deputy mayor. Pendleton's glare bore into Newton. She then directed her eyes to each person seated in the room. "I will not repeat myself. This method of midnight child recruitment will not take place in this city nor in this state." The room grew silent. Assemblywoman Pendleton was angry, yet still confident that all fully understood her position on this matter. She stood up then stormed out of the room. No one spoke for a moment: they allowed the dominating wake of *Madam* Pendleton to ebb from the room.

"Well, I believe we have our marching orders, ladies and gentlemen," said Mayor Fountain. "Personal opinions aside, we have an obligation to our politically challenged constituency. We have to initiate a formal investigation regarding the validity of this school and its practices. If all is as rumored, the school will be legally off-limits to the citizens of Philadelphia. Meeting adjourned." The conference room quickly emptied. There was some muttering regarding the addition of Councilwoman Newton to Assemblywoman Pendleton's "special people" list but it did not appear to bother the new councilwoman.

Al Connell remained in his chair, staring, yet not fully focused on a picture mounted on the wall. "Tomorrow's another day Al," said Mayor Fountain as he walked near the open door. "I'm going to go outside and make a brief statement to the press."

"And to your constituency," said his deputy mayor.

"Oh yes, to them too."

"No bull, be honest. They're frustrated people." Al Connell knew the mayor like the back of his own hand.

"Of course, Al," said Mayor Fountain. "You know me."

Al gave his mayor a fatherly look. *That's the point.* "They're also good people. I'll be along shortly."

The deputy mayor finally got up and made his way to his office where he picked up the phone and proceeded to dial a private number. He was about to give up on the call when he heard the voice of an old friend, the master carpenter.

CHAPTER SIX

Fellyard Beedley sat at his desk and gave considerable thought to the man seated across from him. "Brodrey-boy, we have a problem. I have serious and long-term plans for this academy, for this fine bastion of academic excellence, for the economically challenged." He laced his fingers and leaned in closer. "I need your help. I have been trying to, let's say... introduce new teaching blood into New Passage Academy. When the mahogany bluebloods enter into the world, I want there to be a 'special' attachment to me. It will be teachers such as yourself who will assist me in this area."

"How do you mean that we, that I, will be helping?" Professor Brodrey Toomers did not like where this was going.

"By patience, by change," said Fellyard. "This world is ever-changing. New leaders will be in place in all sectors of society. Most of the students here will meld into this brave new world. I need them to have a commitment to Fellyard Beedley. That commitment will then be transformed into influence—the perfect partner."

"I don't understand. What do you need from me? I'm just a professor here." Fellyard toyed with his pocket watch, admiring its intricate hand-crafted face. He slowly placed the timepiece in his vest pocket and stared at Professor Brodrey Toomers.

"What I need is your vocal assistance, dear professor. When any administrative meeting occurs that addresses a vote for the dismissal of a faculty member, or recruitment of the same, I need you there." Brodrey's eyebrows came together, still confused regarding his specific role expectations. "I still don't know what you want from me."

Fellyard rolled his eyes, his left one taking its time to return to its normal position. "You are one of the brightest minds in our faculty. What I need from you is to vote affirmative; that means yes, Professor Einstein. Vote yes on all issues regarding dismissals and the same regarding faculty recruitment." He paused long enough for the information to sink in. "You see, dear Brodrey, I tend to have a hand in all dismissals or recruitment. I am not certain as to how long the cats will be away, so I need to hasten my play. I intend to identify and then recruit staff who will share certain, shall we say…peculiarities. You know, Brodrey-boy, not unlike yourself, this will eventually guide young troubled minds to me for protection."

Professor Toomers continued to stare at Beedley, wishing that he would quickly finish so he could be on his way. Beedley returned his stare, slightly lowering his head as if receiving Toomers' fearful thoughts. His jaws tightened as he gave further instructions to the distraught professor. "If I need to share some more details, I'll meet you in your home. By the way, I do like what you've done with your den; the curtains are simply beautiful."

To his credit, Toomers did not flinch, even as he lost some blood flow to the skin. He didn't mention or pose the question as to how Fellyard knew of his recent redecorating. What was the point? He had long ago recognized the fact that it was his own evil choices that welcomed the likes of Fellyard and his ilk. Toomers lowered his head, placing it in defeated hands.

"Fine, fine," he said with his head still lowered. "Whatever you need, I'm here." He raised his head to receive an acknowledgement from his guest. The room was empty.

CHAPTER SEVEN

A crowd that consisted mostly of city folk had marched to City Hall to protest the existence of New Passage Academy. Community leaders had gathered the masses to ensure that everyone understood that they were not cattle for social experimentation. There was a special meeting scheduled and the mayor was holding a press conference at five o'clock that afternoon. Before any of the politicians had arrived to the assigned podium area, reporters were working the crowd, attempting to find someone who might be colorful enough for a prime-time interview.

News reporter Synthia Godbold-Pearson was among the television representatives. She and her cameraman, Francis, were surveying the crowd to identify the community leaders. Synthia also made frequent checks on her mobile phone to ensure that she had not missed a call from the office. Earlier she had received a strange voice message regarding New Passage Academy: if there were an opportunity to trump the other news stations, she didn't want to miss it.

"Oh, I know who you are," said a soft voice on her left side. "You're that Godbold-Pearson news lady. Surprised that you would even dirty yourself by being down here with us. Thought you'd be an inside-the-building kinda lady."

Synthia turned to put a face to the soft voice. It was a woman in her mid-fifties, although Synthia couldn't be sure.

"Are you from the area?" she said.

"From what area, lady? I'm a city resident: that should be good enough."

Synthia held the woman's gaze. "Yes, you're right, it should be enough, and it is. Might I have your name?"

"Hey, just talk regular, lady. Don't need no 'might I have' from you. But anyway, my name is Amelia." "Why are you here, Amelia? Are you here to speak for or against special schooling?"

Amelia gave Synthia a long look. At first Synthia believed that she was going to turn and walk away. "Still not sure what 'special school' means," said Amelia. "You gotta remember that to many people, special is just a code word for problem. Could be mental problems, could be physical problems or even problems with the law. Special is a big word that can mean a lot."

Synthia dared a comment. "But Amelia, I know that you understand that there is a problem with certain areas of the city when it comes to public schools."

Amelia's voice began to get a little higher, "Well, I guess I did kinda hear that once. And what has been done about the problem? Nothing. Oh, I guess that's news, huh? All we get is a coat of paint or a change of name like that means it's now somehow different. What's the saying, 'Tuxedo on a pig'? But that don't mean that people can just come in here and do what they want to our children, now does it? Hell, pretty soon they won't be coming in to just take the children; they'll be coming in to take everybody in the house away. Oh, I remembers a little about history."

"But you understand that the city leaders are meeting right now to handle the situation."

"Handle the situation? Lady please. Oh, I'm supposed to do a dance just because some politicians done figured out there is a problem and now they want to figure it all out. You means to tell me that there was not a problem with the schools a year ago?" She rolled her eyes. "Funny, I don't remember seeing you out here with your camera and all last year. Wasn't no problem then? No, I guess not. Ain't never a problem as long as the problem keeps its voice down and don't bother nobody." She began punctuating her words with the point of a finger. "Lady, I really don't know why I'm here. Ain't nothing gonna change, don't nobody really care." More of the crowd gathered to listen to Amelia speak, many murmuring in agreement. Amelia, focused and passionate, didn't even notice them as she pointed an accusatory finger at the municipal edifice.

"What I do know is that I am sick and tired of people all the time telling me what's good for me. Telling me what *Amelia* should do, and how *Amelia* should behave." Amelia's breathing had changed, her chest rising as her shoulders worked to restrain its movement. "Lady, I don't dislike you, but why don't you news folk just go. Just close down the circus!"

"Is that what you think, Amelia?" said Synthia. "That this is all for show?"

"What else is it good for? I'm so sick and tired of you fake intellectuals coming up here all the time telling us about what's good for us. You don't live where we live. We love our community and our people, and we have a dignity of our own. Just because you can explain it better doesn't mean that you're right." The growing crowd gave her energy. "Whatever the problems are, we can fix it for ourselves and by ourselves. Why do people like you always come in on your self-appointed high horses and say how bad we are?"

"Please Amelia, I'm not saying that," said Synthia.

Amelia ignored her. "We don't need no special schools just because we on bad times. Just how the hell do you get off telling some mother that she ain't fit to raise her own just because she can't afford to have an IRA or take vacations in Paris?" Amelia saw people nodding their heads in agreement. "Somebody always thinks that they can do better for someone else, which usually means that they too busy looking down on us ghetto natives. Thinking that we should just be tickled natural pink that someone even remembers to drop a crumb our way; and thinking that anybody can do better than what we're doing for a child." Amelia's eyes swelled with tears that she refused to release. "I can try as hard as I can, but the whole damn world says I'm always doing it wrong—always." Amelia tried to look away, to hide the tears that could no longer be held at bay. It was as if an inner storm had been held steady for years within her weary body. The survivalist exterior that kept her, and many like her safe within her environment, had on this day given up, allowing that which was merely human to reveal itself.

"Miss, whatever the problem is, we can fix it with the kids being at home. Who says that a mother's not fit to raise her own kids? I'll tell you who. The same folks who believe that all we do is lay down and spread our legs to whoever. Don't matter none to animals, does it? I know that's the thinking in there," said Amelia, pointing to City Hall. "And especially in there." She pointed toward the invisible audience within the camera. "Ooh, we should be clapping and be's so happy that somebody's got a school for our human garbage. They want us to be saying, *oh thanks, Mister.* Well, I says, Mister, give me a break. Mister, you can go to hell!"

Synthia, with microphone raised, stood rigid, stilled by Amelia's honest passion. She began to reconnect with some of the frustrations that were lived on a daily basis by her fellow Philadelphians. There was a profound and simple eloquence in Amelia's revelation of her pain. Before Synthia could again speak to Amelia, the woman had turned away and was almost down the street.

CHAPTER EIGHT

Amelia did have more to say and had intended to wait to hear the mayor's speech, but she could not stay any longer. No one in the crowd knew about the long-held struggle that had, for years, battled Amelia's spirit. She still had more to share with Synthia but knew that she could no longer control the emotional surge emerging from a place that she had believed to be secured by time. Her tightly folded pain had become emancipated by the heated confrontation of the past few minutes. Synthia would never know that, even after all these years, Amelia cried from within, cried about a barren womb that had once carried a life. Although compassionate, Synthia was unable to discern the tears left inside that had silently turned to poison. Poison soon partnered with time to slowly erode both body and spirit.

Few people would recall a sixteen-year-old Amelia who had been counseled regarding what would be best for her and her child. She was repeatedly and thoroughly admonished that her household and her world could not compassionately receive an infant. But Amelia harbored strong sensibilities about the world, as well as her own spirit. Even at sixteen she firmly embraced her heart's whispers, which affirmed the profound affection and love that she held for the baby in her womb. The young teenager finally gave in and did the "right thing" by not allowing a child to be a burden to a silly high school student. Amelia remembered being showered with praise for becoming more of a grown up, having made a mature decision. None of her concerned counselors had returned to console Amelia when the botched abortion had left her unable to ever bring a child into the world. Twenty-eight years later, Amelia still felt haunted by the child that never was. Some days she mused on how she might get a call from her daughter, might be asked if she were available for a mother-daughter get-together. Amelia was familiar with others who had also done "what is best," some more than once. Most never seemed to give it another thought.

From a distance Amelia thought that she heard the voice of the reporter lady calling to her. She quickened her steps and turned the corner, finding refuge within the musty coolness of a local market. Amelia had almost settled her mind until she heard the voice of a woman coming from behind.

Damn, news lady, how did you find me here? It wasn't Synthia. The voice belonged to a young, pregnant woman trying to access the detergent aisle. Amelia muttered, "Sorry." She bit her lip and turned toward the market's exit. This time her tears behaved as trained, seeping inward. Amelia had successfully resealed her emotional chest. Taking one last glance toward the glowing young mother-to-be, she ignored the flash of pain in her abdomen and slowly walked out of the market into the welcoming distraction of city life.

CHAPTER **NINE**

Brodrey Toomers was a Professor of Applied Physics at New Passage Academy. He had been recruited in 1993 by the academy's faculty search committee. Prior to his recruitment, Toomers was actually quite comfortable with his former position as a professor at a prestigious university in Georgia. Originally a native of Philadelphia, Pennsylvania, he and his wife had enjoyed the people and culture of the City of Brotherly Love. It was therefore quite a surprise to her when he had accepted the offer to relocate to Georgia. At the time Toomers did not appear to be quite himself. She did not press him regarding the decision to explore the warmer climate of the southern state. He was well-respected in his field, and her assumption was that other institutions placed significant financial value on his potential contribution to the faculty.

When subsequently contacted by New Passage Academy, Professor Toomers initially declined the generous offer to leave the comfortable confines of his post in Georgia. Two months later, he made an inquiry to New Passage Academy, hoping that the offer was still on the table. Unbeknownst to his potential employers, Toomers' wife had slowly grown suspicious of her husband's peculiar sexual appetites. She threatened to expose him and leave him. Toomer had been extremely careful as well as infrequent in his indulgences, yet unknowingly, he had still provided clues. Afraid of losing his source of income, especially when confronted with financial obligations toward his now unforgiving wife, he contacted the unsuspecting New Passage Academy.

Initially, the relationship had proven to be a wonderful experience for Brodrey Toomers. The philosophy and the resources of the institution had shown the professor that the mind of a child was indeed worthy of academic commitment. Toomers had witnessed the various transitional stages that the new students went through as they rediscovered the true intellectual beauty which defined them. Toomers was also surrounded by a group of dedicated and professional peers who embraced a commitment to the long-term objectives of the academy.

CHAPTER **TEN**

Musk hung in the stilled air of the Greater Mountains Church of Christ's basement. All who were present gathered in a storage room. Reverend Randolph Sydney sat at the head of the table, firmly gripping his signature gold pen. To his left was Deacon Bazemore Crawley, whose tightly buttoned shirt produced a high torque pressure point at his waistline. Included among the assembled church leaders were Deaconess Sapphire Pennywell, who despite possessing a nice figure for her age, found that her scattered-tooth smile kept most suitors at bay; and Sister Beatrice Tatum. She held no actual title but was a long-term, significant contributor to the congregation and was therefore indulged. To her credit, she was a faithful and consistent asset at committee functions. There was also Minister Patrick Benton, the newest member, who was still finding his place within the congregation. He, however, knew better than to jump full-force into one issue or another.

"We just can't ignore the situation regarding our dear Sister Snowden and her new boyfriend," said Reverend Sydney.

"We don't even know that he actually is a boyfriend," said Sister Tatum. "I mean, just having a man visit from time to time doesn't make him a boyfriend, not even a lover. Not speaking from experience, of course." All eyes turned toward Sister Tatum.

"Okay, we'll just say 'friend' for now," said Reverend Sydney as he shot a raised eyebrow toward Sister Tatum. "But the fact of the matter is that something is wrong—very wrong." With pleading eyes, he looked toward Deaconess Pennywell. "Someone should really go over to her house and speak to her."

"Why yes, a couple of you should make that trip." Deaconess Pennywell did not want the responsibility. Her mouth remained mercifully clenched, sparing all the enameled vision of Tom Sawyer's partially painted fence. Reverend Sydney smiled at his failed attempt to separate himself from the assignment. He knew that he would have to be a part of this particularly awkward expedition.

"You're right; it would be nice if a couple of people went, besides…" All conversation was suspended as a song from the upstairs choir rehearsal rapidly took a different turn, as well as tone. It wasn't a problem with the musician, but of the attempt by the soloist to convey that *Jesus is the sweetest name I know.* The pain was doubled by the fact that the soloist was the first lady of the church, Darmela Sydney. Everyone sitting in the storage room could almost feel the struggle of Tyrus, the organist, as he futilely fought to find the right key—any key. As soon as the correct note was found, Sister Sydney had somehow leaped into a new one.

"Oh, dear Jesus," slipped from the lips of Deacon Crawley. Before he attempted to return to the topic at hand, he stole a fearful glance in the reverend's direction to see if his pastor had heard the whispered faux pas. Reverend Sydney was kind and astute enough to pretend that he had not heard the comment. *Somehow, I'm gonna have to tell my lovely wife to simply step away from the mike,* thought the good reverend, the irony of pastoring such a heavenly flock only to catch hell at home not escaping him. *Help me Jesus.*

"You say something, pastor?"

"Oh no, just remembered something I have to do. Let's return to the business at hand."

Everyone stiffened as the organ once again started up. They exhaled when they realized that the director had changed the song, complete with a more talented soloist.

"Let's not dwell on this unpleasant issue," said Reverend Sydney. "Sister Tatum, will you and Deaconess Pennywell join me for a visit to Sister Snowden's home?"

"Yes, reverend, that will be fine, but what will we say?" Deaconess Pennywell was being polite, but she really did not want to be bothered.

Reverend Sydney spoke slowly. "What we need to say to Sister Snowden is that we believe that her new boyfriend, or friend, can do her no good. We'll be very clear on the fact that it is not about us interfering in her business, but that we hold a great fear regarding her well-being."

"But can we be sure, reverend?" said Sister Tatum. "Just what do we actually know?"

"Well, we know that he bought the old Fremont house," said Deacon Crawley. "That place has been sitting for years. Nobody wanted to touch it."

"Actually, he fixed it up really nice," said Minister Benton.

"Yes, yes he did, Brother Minister," said Reverend Sydney. "It's just those weird lawn ornaments. They just don't... don't feel right." No one knew much regarding Sister Snowden's mysterious friend. All they truly knew was that he was not local. Why did he choose this neighborhood? Was there some family association? It was anyone's guess. There was nothing wrong with being a new face; it was just that his face was rarely seen. Few could admit to ever having a real encounter with the evasive man.

"Actually, I told Reverend Sydney that my wife and I ran into him one night," said Deacon Bazemore. "We were at the convenience store and he was kinda standing outside of the store just watching people as they pumped their gas. When I approached him to say hello, he just looked at me funny with an odd grin. He said something under his breath and then walked toward the gas pumps. Now I'm trying to figure out why he's standing in front of the store if his car is in front of a gas pump."

"You didn't see him get in a car?" said Deaconess Pennywell. The question appeared to catch Deacon Bazemore off-guard.

"You know, come to think of it, I didn't. Funny, I never even thought about it before now. I really can't remember where he went."

"I did go by the man's home to drop off a church flyer," said Reverend Sydney. "As I drove up, I saw him in his front yard pushing soil up against his lawn fixtures; still can't figure out why. I was thinking that it was a real good time to chat. You know, somehow it's a little easier for men to have good conversations when they got their sleeves rolled up. When I stepped out of my car, he stops working. Now he was kneeling with his back to me and he never turned around. He just stopped working." Reverend Sydney stopped to think, his eyes looking ahead, but at no one at the table. "The man never looked over his shoulder, never turned his head. Even still, I felt that he could see me, knew that I was there. Don't ask me how. I just knew. Before I could say anything, he gets up—he still hasn't turned his head—and walks directly into his house."

"But don't we need some kind of proof?" said Minister Benton. "Can we just recommend something just because it doesn't feel right?"

"Yes we can, young man, we're the church—amen."

CHAPTER ELEVEN

Comfortably reclining in her patio chair, Georgia Matthews surveyed the animated beauty of her garden. Her thoughts were not as comfortable. She wondered if she had done the right thing by contacting Synthia Godbold-Pearson regarding New Passage Academy. Mrs. Matthews harbored mixed emotions but was acting on a call that she had received earlier from a former student.

A distraught Nora Sanford had contacted Mrs. Matthews several days ago. After the initial pleasantries had been exhausted, Nora had spoken of long sleepless nights with thoughts that not all was well with her son. Nora had explained that LeDain had been at the academy for over a year. Even though she strongly missed him, all appeared to be going well. Nora's first six month visit with LeDain had been brief; still, she was surprised at how much he had progressed. She almost didn't recognize the young man who now addressed her in a sophisticated manner. Nora marveled over how informed LeDain was about current events.

There had also been an additional visit two months ago so LeDain could attend the funeral of his brother Jared. Jared had become one of the city's murder victim statistics. He and his friend had decided to attend a late-night party in a different part of town. All was going well at the party until Jared had approached a young lady. Her attraction was magnified by the taut, pink top that boldly spelled out her sexy status. Some of the locals didn't appreciate Jared's romantic, albeit juvenile, overtures. No one really remembered what happened, only that shots rang out. Jared and his friend ran outside. They had gotten only as far as the sidewalk when Jared fell abruptly, mortally wounded with a bullet in his back.

At Jared's services, Nora had held LeDain close throughout the day. Her initial thoughts were to withdraw LeDain from the academy, to keep him close at all times. The tearful glimpses at the body of Jared, a body that would never contain any more speech or movement, once again altered her thoughts. A mother's eyes that had once observed the innocent rocking of an infant's bassinet was now forced to bare witness to her child's final vessel of rest. Nora's motherly love met that same mother's fear. She resolved that this pain would not be repeated, that LeDain would place the flowers on her casket.

Shortly after LeDain had returned to the school, Nora told Mrs. Matthews that she began to be troubled by disturbing dreams. The dreams saw LeDain calling out to her for help. A couple of times, her dreams contained the voice of a man who called out to her son. It was strange: the man's voice had almost a farm-hand type simplicity to it. It seemed like the man was concerned about the boy and meant him no harm.

Nora had contacted the school via a private line relay system that put her in touch with the Academy's liaison counselor. The counselor assured her that all was well with LeDain at the school, and that she had no need to worry. Her fears, for the moment, were assuaged. Nora tried to put any problems out of her mind and blame it all on the ongoing issues in her life. Her employers were experiencing some financial turmoil and had therefore cut everyone's hours. She still owed money toward Jared's funeral bills. For the moment she was feeling very grateful for New Passage Academy.

About a week later, she received a call at about two in the morning. When she picked up the phone, she could hear the phone hissing but no one was speaking. All of her motherly intuition told her that it was LeDain. She just had to get to him quickly. But how? Nora went to City Hall to register a complaint. She wanted to speak with someone with political influence. It was only when Nora had threatened to convey her frustrations to the newspaper that a clerk promised to get it into the hands of Nora's councilman.

Nora's mental fatigue had led her to her favorite teacher from middle school. This compassionate and supportive teacher had struggled with teaching Nora basic math but Georgia Matthews had observed that Nora liked to read and always had some sort of a riddle or puzzle-type book. Nora was thirteen years old when

Georgia Matthews sat her down and opened up one of her riddle books.

"I see that math is kinda of hard for you, Nora," she said.

"Yes, Mrs. Matthews, I just can't seem to follow the rules of the numbers and all."

"It can get tricky sometimes. I used to have problems when I was a little girl."

"Math was hard for you, Mrs. Matthews?"

"Yes, Nora, teachers weren't always so smart." She leaned and whispered. "And sometimes we're still not so smart." They both laughed. "I see that you always have your riddle book with you," said Mrs. Matthews.

"Yes, ma'am, I like to play the tricky games and things."

"Oh, I see that you do. And you seem to be very good at it. Now, Nora, solving riddles means that you can step back and think through problems. Let me tell you a secret: math is nothing but riddles without words. For you, we're going to stop calling it math. We're going to call it Nora's number riddles."

By the end of the month, Nora's grades had greatly improved as well as her confidence in math. She and Mrs. Matthews kept in touch throughout her high school years. Every now and then she would still receive a postcard from Mrs. Matthews who had become a principal, and was now retired.

Nora needed help. One of her fellow church members, who was also a retired teacher, was able to put her in touch with her former teacher. A very grateful and relieved Nora eventually found Mrs. Matthews and shared with her the lengthy story of New Passage Academy, expressing her fears for her son.

Georgia Matthews continued her quiet reflection among her lovely hibiscus and fragrant camellia garden. She had heard rumors of New Passage Academy some years back. Strange how it was once again at her doorstep. Mrs. Matthews had patiently listened to Nora speak regarding her current fears about her son. She told Mrs. Matthews that she did not have a lot of information or paperwork on the school, but that she would send what she had.

It was this vague information that Mrs. Matthews had shipped, via overnight service, to newswoman Synthia Godbold-Pearson. Perhaps it was indeed time for New Passage Academy to come to the light. Mrs. Matthews just wondered if she had done the right thing.

The sound of a car pulling in the driveway brought her back to the present. A white BMW came to a stop and Mrs. Matthews stood up to greet her guest.

CHAPTER TWELVE

Sitting in the midst of Mrs. Georgia Matthews' well-maintained patio was Synthia Godbold-Pearson. Mrs. Matthews had just returned from her kitchen with a decorative pitcher filled with iced tea. Synthia watched her host pour the icy beverage into two frosted glasses. Mrs. Matthews also set down a small tray of homemade gingerbread. Always reminding herself that she made a living out of being in front of the camera, Synthia respectfully declined the cookies. As she lifted her glass to take a sip, a devious wind arose, folding the distinctive molasses-rich aroma of cookies to her nostrils. Synthia impressed herself with her mental resolve to still leave the sugar crusted—hmm, she hadn't noticed that before—oversized cookies on the silver tray. One last glance at the thick cookies reminded Synthia that it was a homemade delicacy, void of any of those ugly preservatives. *Ah, but that probably means more butter and such; therefore, it's still not a good idea.* Synthia's last culinary thought was a reminder from her mother to not offend your host. *Enough of this*, she thought. *Just do your job girl.* She picked up a cookie.

"You have such an impressive garden, Mrs. Matthews. With this iced tea and delicious cookies, I could just sit a spell, let the day pass on by."

Mrs. Matthews laughed. "You just sit all you want, honey. A garden and a wonderful day, sometimes it is just made for being still." She crossed her legs.

"You ever wonder about flowers, Mrs. Pearson? I mean, why are flowers so important to us? Flowers are required in many of our rites of passage such as births, deaths, and weddings. Why do we need flowers? Do they speak of newness, health, vitality, freshness, or purity? Perhaps they speak to the human body; a reminder of our relationship with earth and its elements—earth, wind, and fire."

"*Blessed are the children.* Uh, sorry," said Synthia. "You know that you can't even hint about my Earth Wind and Fire, let alone just come out and say it."

Mrs. Matthews gave a warm laugh. "Yes, I guess that was too easy," she said. "And I ain't mad at you. Actually, that song is very appropriate; you know that it's actually a prayer?"

"A prayer?" said Synthia. "What do you mean? If we're talking about the same song I used to shake my little groove thing to!"

"Who didn't?" Synthia gave a polite yet doubtful look.

"You young people see gray and think that's how some of us have always been. You don't think that I used to have a groove thing, or a man that liked the way it grooved?" She raised an eyebrow toward Synthia. "But seriously, the song is called *Devotion*, and it speaks of the same: devotion, meditation, and prayer. Many people have never really listened to the simple yet profound words. Besides, after 'blessed are the children,' the next line is 'praise the teacher'." She winked. Still smiling, she reached down to pick up a starter plant that she had been nurturing. "I believe that God gave us flowers just to act as a stoplight along the way."

"What do you mean? Something like you'd better stop and smell the roses kinda of talk?" said Synthia.

"Well, kind of…exactly. I dare anyone to just simply race through a meadow that has been fragrantly showered with the color brilliance of God's blessings." Mrs. Matthews looked up at Synthia. "Yes, I guess it can sound corny and all, but flowers do move us, change us." She could see that she had Synthia's attention. "Years ago, I would bear witness to hell on earth from the way the children would be acting in school. I would swear that that would be my last day, and I'd find a job elsewhere. Later I would come home to my garden and just sit awhile. Pretty soon my mind would ease down, my thoughts become less raw as the flowers completed their reasonably priced hypnotherapy." She closed her eyes long enough to enjoy the passing breeze. "Flowers also remind me of the people in my life, some here, some that have gone on. I reflect on certain periods in my life, good or bad. Some days I just close my eyes and inhale a bit of God's fragrant recipe. After a few slow breaths, I'm transported back to being a little girl, playing in the backyard with my older sisters. Oh, they are both gone now, but every now and then I can still inhale their laughter."

Synthia didn't have a lot of free time to spend at Mrs. Matthew's home. She began to seek a moment in Mrs. Matthews's conversation when she might diplomatically interrupt, bring her back to the point. However, Synthia soon found that her own thoughts had begun to drift. The bouquet from the surrounding flowers had begun to reach her. Her eyes were drawn to the fluttering dance of two butterflies who vied for the same flower, even though there were plenty of petals to go around. Having already surrendered her sight and smell, Synthia released her own childhood memories, stimulated by Mrs. Matthew's childhood story.

Synthia was an eight-year-old girl at First Baptist Vacation Bible School. All the children were assembled on the new lush-green grass that was liberally speckled with dandelions. The girls had picked a handful of the dandelions and were performing the obligatory blowing of the soft thistles. Close by, a few boys in the group were creeping up on a small grasshopper. They grinned in anticipation—all were one in their nonverbal conspiracy to place the insect on the lap of one of the unsuspecting girls. Even Sister Sculliard, the Sunday School Teacher, had eased back on the firm discipline that had made her famous. Today, at this moment, in God's garden all was well.

"Don't you agree, Mrs. Pearson?"

Synthia's thoughts hurried back to current times. She only caught the end of Mrs. Matthews's question. "I'm sorry, Mrs. Matthews, I didn't hear all of what you said. Forgive me."

"That's all right, young lady, I warned you, didn't I?" They both smiled. "I'm not so old that I don't know that you're a busy woman, Mrs. Pearson. I won't hold you up with any more garden thoughts. Let's talk education, shall we?" Mrs. Matthews reached down again and brought forth a thick envelope. "In here is additional information that I have on New Passage Academy. This and the items that I mailed to you should be enough to put you on the doorstep of the school." She pulled in a deep breath. "Let me also share a story regarding this mysterious place." She used the back of her forefinger to absentmindedly stroke the soft leaf of the plant.

"Many years ago I had heard rumors of the school, but there was nothing that could even marginally confirm its presence. To be honest, I was at first very upset regarding what I did hear. That's why I guess that many people wouldn't even begin to believe in its existence. I mean, how could...who would give up their child? Naw, it was all just a teacher's lounge myth. You know, like better pay." Synthia smiled at her last comment as she reached for another cookie. *I'll skip dinner.*

Mrs. Matthews face changed from its pleasant smile, becoming taut, and disturbingly pensive. "You know, I had a little granddaughter once. She would be about twenty-four years old now. She would probably be bugging me to baby-sit her little one," she said, with a trace of pain in her tone. She was determined not to be overcome with the thoughts of her precious seed, a seed that had never flowered into life's fullness.

"I was principal at the time; my daughter was working second shift, as a nurse will do sometimes. I'd have Keyanna in the office with me. Even had the custodian move one of the little desks to my office so she'd have a place to do her drawings and such. We had an after-school program, so I'd let Keyanna join with the other kids. Everything was working out just fine." Synthia wondered if she should spare Mrs. Matthews by trying to change the subject, but something in her understood that she needed to be heard.

"It was early spring; the children were outside playing. They were being watched by the teachers and other helpers. The neighborhood wasn't the best, but still, there was never any problem around the kids and such." She looked at Synthia. "Yeah, children and old folks used to be kinda sacred so to speak, nobody bothered them. It didn't matter how messed up you were as a man or woman, there was still some sense of respect, or boundaries towards certain people or places. The winos would stop to let you pass, even tip their hat. I remember how we used to chastise the winos. I'd take 'em back in a minute in exchange of these vicious crack heads we got now." She paused as if to collect her thoughts. "Well, anyway, I had just finished up on something for the school system's superintendent when, over the cheerful yells of the children, I heard several shots ring out." Ms. Matthews paused, her thoughts becoming more of an anchor than a memory. Synthia could almost see her back become bowed, pressed by an invisible weight.

"At first I yelled for Timmons, the custodian, then I quickly remembered the children outside. Playful chatter had abruptly turned into horrible shrieks. Immediately an icy rope became lashed about my heart as I thought of Keyanna. I sprang up and raced toward the playground area. When I reached the double exit doors, they stood as steel monsters, almost as sentinels at hell's gate. I pushed forward but the door wouldn't open. I think that part of me understood that as long as the door didn't open, whatever evil thing that was causing the screams was not yet real, could not be real until the doors...until they opened." Her eyes glossed over. "I gave three feeble lunges. My heart couldn't take it no more, so I leaned in and the door flew open with ease. All I can remember seeing was the still form of my little Keyanna. She was on the ground, but I could see the blood trail from where someone had taken her from the sliding board. Strangely, her eyes were still bright, although they looked at nothing."

She pushed her hair away from her eyes. "I went toward her, but couldn't reach her. I didn't realize that my legs had given way and that I was reaching for her while on bended knees. Only thing that I recall is that I did finally make it to my feet, only to faint away on the dusty ground."

Synthia had closed her eyes long ago. She wanted to give Mrs. Matthews her privacy, as well as a attempt to suppress her own tears. She realized that her heart was beating faster, attempting to will the story into a happier outcome. Mrs. Matthews was slowly rocking in the way that all grandmothers do when family sorrows bid them good morning.

"I later found out about the young boy who had done the shooting. The boy was shooting at someone who he thought had stolen his radio—a damn thirty dollar radio." She nodded as if it was still hard to believe. "Fact of the matter was that he was once selected by the New Passage Academy, but his mother changed her mind because she didn't want to lose him. Lost him in the end anyway, for about the same length of time. You see, he got eight to ten years in juvenile corrections. Only thing is, when he finally came home, he was so strung out, so weak in body and mind." She refilled Synthia's and her glasses with tea. "He was too young for prison, and it just ate him up. I lost my baby, that mother lost her son. Just what if she had said yes all those years ago? Would my little Keyanna still be alive? Hell, they might even be married to each other. One decision can change so much, so much." Mrs. Matthews looked at Synthia, not even caring about the tears in her eyes. "I'm sorry, Mrs. Pearson. I don't mean to put my troubles on your doorstep. You just came by for some information. It's just that as I look at you, I can see my Keyanna. How she might be working for you at the TV station or something. You two might even be friends and getting your hair done together."

They sat there for a while, agreeing in silence. The garden flowers were listening. They went to work, offering their collective expressions of comfort to weighted spirits.

Finally, Mrs. Matthews stood up, understanding that Synthia's compassionate sense of courtesy would not allow her to make the first move.

"I have truly enjoyed meeting you, as well as our conversation. I hope that this is not the last time that you will share my garden with me."

"The pleasure was truly all mine," said Synthia. "I thank you for not just informing me about the school, but for reminding me that I do need to sit and inhale the day. This was indeed time well spent. I would be sorely disappointed if you do not invite me back. Next time, I promise you that I will let you have one of your own cookies."

The ladies hugged and walked arm in arm until Synthia reached the driveway. Synthia got in her car and waved again as she drove away. Mrs. Matthews turned and walked back to her garden. She kneeled down amongst the flowers. Bending forward, she eased a few of the willing petals to her face and inhaled the life memory of her little Keyanna.

CHAPTER THIRTEEN

Synthia had just enjoyed a light lunch at one of her favorite restaurants. Her deepened thoughts caused her to lose track of time. She paid her bill and hurried through the restaurant door. Her thoughts were still on the package that remained nestled in her arms. *Could this be some sort of hoax?* It just didn't seem quite possible. The package contents and the subsequent visit with Mrs. Matthews still had her perplexed. Mentally multitasking for a moment, Synthia lost track of where she had parked her BMW. Refocusing on her surroundings, Synthia began to sense that she was being watched. Though not one for being superstitious or paranoid, still something was unsettling her. Snap out of it girl, she thought as she applied a tighter grip around the oversized office envelope. *Get a little disturbing information, and now you're turning into Miss Creepy World USA.*

Fellyard Beedley sipped his coffee, patiently waiting for Synthia to leave. It didn't bother him that his beverage was no longer hot, nor was he upset that his quarry did not appear to be in a hurry. Through many years, Fellyard had perfected the art of patience. It had served him well regarding many a subject.

There was no problem with the waitress regarding his small order, even as he remained sitting for a lengthy period of time. In fact, she was all too happy that the odd man had not gestured for her to stop by his table. Fellyard had the feeling that if he simply got up and walked out of the restaurant without paying, there would be no one chasing after him. His leaving would be more than enough payment.

A dusty, charcoal-hued fedora sat on Fellyard's head as he continued his solemn and distant watch over Synthia Godbold-Pearson. His head jerked slightly as he noticed that she had waved the waitress over to her table to pay the check. As Synthia got up and made her way to the exit, Fellyard dropped a few crumpled dollars on the table and casually strolled toward the same exit.

He never saw the waitress come over to the table with intentions of pocketing her well-deserved tip. Instead she used her table rag to quickly swipe the oily dollars into her waste bin with all the other discarded items. Her financial needs did not match her unexplained loathing to touch anything that had lingered with such a disturbing man.

Upon exiting the restaurant, Fellyard smirked as he spotted Synthia walking down the avenue. Her steps were somewhat indecisive, implying that she had yet to make up her mind concerning her direction. *How easy it would be to ease this distracted woman into the path of a moving truck,* thought Fellyard. He quickened his steps to shorten the distance between the two. He slowed his pace as he remembered that he had others to do this type of work. A city bus, filled mostly with summer students from the community college, turned the corner and was headed toward them. The occupants of the bus were unusually loud, even for students. They cursed and threatened the poor bus driver as if he were responsible for the faulty air-conditioning unit. The bus driver was angry and cursed them back. He reminded his charges that unlike them, he was not getting off at nearby stops but had to drive all afternoon in the hot box. His eyes left the road many times as he honed in on the loudest protesters. The bus was drawing closer to the vicinity of Synthia. Fellyard was entertaining a lethal rush to her blindside when he noticed that she had turned to the side. He initially believed that she had sensed him and had turned to confront him. Then he noticed that she was speaking to someone in a limousine.

"Damn, who's watching over this woman?" He abruptly turned and walked the other way.

The stranger who had watched Fellyard and Chadric as they conversed near the cars was also observing Synthia's activity. His perch on the bus stop bench offered him a reasonably effective view of all passersby. The stranger's funds allowed no restaurant table but it afforded him a pretzel from one of the street vendors. His curiosity arose when he saw the late model limousine stop and startled Synthia. He was even more intrigued when she accepted a ride. *This woman is going to be hard to get to,* he thought. He slowly stood and quietly melted into the city.

CHAPTER **FOURTEEN**

No sooner had Synthia gathered her thoughts and confirmed the whereabouts of her parked car, than her heart once again plunged as a strong voice called out to her and almost made her leap from her skin.

"Excuse me, Miss Godbold?" Synthia glanced toward the firm voice and found the gentle face of a distinguished gentleman who peered out from the back window of the limousine.

"Please, Miss Godbold…oh, that's right, it's Mrs. Pearson, isn't it? I am so forgetful at times. My sincere congratulations to you and your new husband. He's a good man."

Synthia was not one to get too close to a stranger, but something about this kind face suggested no danger, and besides, she was still a reporter. She found her voice and answered the man.

"Actually, the name is Godbold-Pearson. Do we know each other?"

"Forgive my ill manners, my dear, and allow me to introduce myself: my name is Franklin, Joseph Franklin, at your service. Please, may we speak for a moment?"

Synthia again eyed the limousine and its passenger. "I have an office that you can call if you need an appointment." In the most polite fashion, Franklin pretended that he had not even heard.

"If we can, perhaps, just meet in that office building the next block over, Mrs. Pearson, I won't hold you long. I would not be so dramatic or unaware of current social dangers that I would actually ask you to enter a stranger's car." Synthia's posture remained cautious. Franklin's voice went a little lower as he added, "It will help you in such matters as, shall we say, private education?" He had her full attention. Franklin continued.

53

"My corporate office is much more conducive to conversation and we will be much more comfortable there. You can sign in at the security desk if you like. That way you'll feel better about meeting with a total stranger in his office."

Synthia glanced at her watch and then at the stone-faced driver. The professional in her rose to the occasion. "Tell you what... Mr. Franklin, is it? Let me call this meeting into my office and we will ride together to your office. What's the exact address of the building?"

Synthia relayed the meeting information to her office while Franklin patiently thumbed through a weekly financial magazine. Synthia entered the ultra-plush surroundings of the late model limousine. The rose petal smoothness of the leather seats seemed to wrap around Synthia's body. She dared to lean her head back and swore to sell the house to *get one of these*. She enjoyed the limousine until they pulled up in front of a stately, beige-stoned edifice complete with a uniformed doorman.

"Good afternoon, Mr. Franklin," said Carlos, the young doorman.

"Why good afternoon to you, Carlos. How's the new, little Carlos doing?"

"Just fine, sir. Just fine." Although only about five-foot seven in size, Carlos appeared to grow a foot at the mention of his newborn son.

"Careful, Carlos, you might pop a button or two if you stick out your chest too far." Mr. Franklin smiled. The encounter did not escape Synthia's observation. Who was this gentleman who not only had an office in the building, but thought it not beneath his station to chat with the doorman?

They walked toward a R*estricted Access Only* area, away from the main elevators. Synthia hesitated, then stopped cold.

I don't believe that I have the proper clearance to go there," she said, looking at the sign.

"That's quite all right, my dear, you have me. You see, this is my building." It took Synthia a moment to realize that her mouth was open. She almost had it closed when around the corner came a large security officer. He wore no cheap badge that declared him to be an employee of a typical *Yellow Pages* security company: this gentleman bore the presence of a high-end private security entity. His attire was not a gray store-rack job but a tailored designer suit that fitted firmly, yet loosely enough to effectively secure a discreet weapon or two. The confident and panther-like movement of the man let Synthia know that the use of any weapon was not usually required: most disagreements would not get that far.

A surprisingly warm smile came from the security expert's face as he opened the elevator door and held it for them. Synthia took note of the elevator's exquisite interior as the distinctive saxophone presence of John Coltrane melodically filled the space. *Who is this man and just what manner of conversation awaits me?* Synthia was too curious.

What impressed Synthia even more was the non-pretentious persona of her host. Joseph Franklin was obviously wearing an expensively tailored suit, yet his posture did not match that of an Ivory Tower club member. She quietly listened as he joked with Terrence, his private security officer, making sarcastic yet friendly remarks regarding Terrence's increasing waistline—a lie. *Um, looks ultra firm to me,* thought Synthia, *he needs Taylea here for an official inspection complete with commentary.* Immediately, Synthia's muscles tensed when she realized that she had probably held her glance too long toward the officer's waistline. Tension turned to blushing as she quickly recalled what was just below the waistline. Her mind began to play with her: *Maybe now he thinks that I'm looking there. But I wasn't so why should I react? But if I turn away now, it'll look like I'm guilty—oh damn!*

"*American Idol* is something I just can't understand," said Franklin.

Huh? Where did that come from? thought Synthia.

"I mean, think about it." He gestured with his hands. "We've completely redefined just what an idol is suppose to be. What do you think?" Synthia wasn't sure if he was talking to her or to Terrence. "Besides, if I were a terrorist or something, I'd schedule a strike just as those hundred-thousand should-be-working or should-be-studying people were making their multiple voting calls. I mean, communications would scramble to a standstill!"

"Well, to tell you the truth," said Synthia, "I don't get a chance to see it much. I'm usually too busy preparing for the next day of work."

"Ah, here we are," said Franklin as the elevator's chime indicated its arrival at the executive floor. Terrence kept his distance as Synthia and Franklin entered the mahogany double doors of a massive office. She turned and started to say thank you to him, only to find no one there.

"Oh, Terrence quickly goes his own way," said Franklin, smiling. "He's silent but deadly. The school kids that visit usually laugh when I say that. Please, Mrs. Pearson, have a seat. Make yourself comfortable."

"I'm sorry, Mr. Franklin. Please don't think of me as rude." Synthia gestured about the room. "This office, the security, this building, I mean…just who are you? I'm a reporter; I know a little something about the power people in this city, but you, sir, are a mystery."

"Why thank you, Mrs. Pearson."

"Synthia, please."

"Splendid, Synthia! Call me Joseph. It is so much more pleasant to discard with formalities, isn't it? Oh, I know that there's a time and place for such things but it's much more relaxed when the tie can be loosened."

Synthia made herself comfortable on the Italian leather sofa while Franklin ignored the high-back Rimini chair and perched himself on the edge of an oversized ottoman.

"Mrs., I mean, Synthia, the reason I said thank you to your mystery man statement is not that I'm trying to be facetious. It is only because my intent is to be anonymous in this city. I am sure that many get a good kick out of having their names in the paper or being on the top of the must-have guest lists. That's okay, to each his own. But my personal joys are not grounded in the expectations or adoration of people whose primary goal is superficial, the worship of the limelight." He let that statement linger for a moment.

"Oh, don't get me wrong, I'm no prude or hypocrite. I do like fine things. It's just that I like things because I like them, not because it is the in thing to have. Neither do I purchase items just so I can ensure that others know that they are in my possession. I'd still trade a black-tie luncheon for a leisurely walk in the park; one meets so many interesting people there." For a moment Franklin peered toward the ceiling as if recalling a certain moment. "There is great enjoyment from a meal that is prepared by a gifted gourmet chef. Just don't forget the unequalled taste of a hot dog, partially burned at a family cookout. You see my dear, there are many enjoyments that I would lose by being a social monstrosity. Therefore, I yet remain," Franklin glanced around the room for effect, "A man of mystery." He leaned back and enjoyed a hearty laugh.

"Here I am saying these things to a newswoman, an anchor newswoman at that. The news and spotlight is what you do!" Synthia shared the laugh, very much at ease with her host.

"No, it's all right. Yes I do report the news and many times people are the news." Her voice lowered. "But I do know what you mean about different enjoyments. I'm not going to lie, I like being recognized and all that. Part of that was the job's allure. But sometimes there is nothing like sitting by yourself in a quiet room while wearing your favorite pair of old pajamas and sipping a large mug of cocoa."

"With marshmallows I trust," said Franklin with a stuffy British accent for added effect.

Synthia didn't miss a beat, returning the accent: "Why yes, my good fellow, only with marshmallows, is there any other civilized way?"

CHAPTER **FIFTEEN**

The People's View News Station hired a fresh-faced Synthia Godbold. She was employed to mainly handle the office needs of the other journalists but the ambitious novice knew of only one speed: full. Whatever was required, Synthia handled without complaint. All the while she was learning every aspect of the news business and she was soon given the responsibilities of being a field reporter. She quickly became popular for her tenacity in getting the stories that most other reporters were either missing or just didn't register on their respective "glitzy" meters. An early Sunday morning program, *Meet Your Neighbor*, that no one else really wanted, turned into an ongoing feature for an appreciative Synthia. The show's popularity increased dramatically and Synthia was soon tested as an anchorwoman on the early evening news. Synthia's quick wit and sharp mind quickly erased her probationary status, and she was given the job on a permanent basis. Long hours and devoted studying soon made Synthia a competent anchorwoman. She was sought after as a personality for various community events and functions. One function, in particular, was the Annual Men's Cook-off Gala. It was this event that placed her in the life of Chadric Pearson.

Chadric Pearson was the owner of a highly successful communications firm. The business had enjoyed phenomenal growth, even during the market's cold spells. While making inquiries regarding Chadric's selection of spices for his sparerib rub, Synthia failed to realize that she had spent a good portion of her rounding time at Chadric's table. It wasn't until Francis, her cameraman, brought this to her attention that she realized she had abandoned her famous stick-and-move credo. Synthia reluctantly moved onto the more neglected chefs but frequently caught herself stealing glances toward Chadric's table.

"Hmm, seems like our good brother chef is working some strong spices, eh, Synthia." Francis raised a brow.

"Who?" Synthia was hoping that her attraction wasn't so obvious.

"Needn't be so coy with me, lady. Spices are what gets the nose open. Yesiree buddy, my sister's nose be wide open." Synthia playfully poked her fist at the Francis.

"Francis, you can kiss my—"

"And you're live." He nudged her shoulder, thinking on his feet. Synthia momentarily launched into a serious but pleasant on-the-air face. She quickly recognized that the camera was still pointing down and Francis' finger was in the gotcha position.

"Oh, I owe you big-time fella."

"You don't owe me anything, honey, but what you should do is to fix your hair from your eyes, because you—"

"Oh no, fool me once...and that's all you get because there's not gonna be a next—"

"Excuse me," the steady voice came from directly behind her. "Excuse me, Ms. Godbold, I don't mean to be forward or rude, but please allow me to give you my business card." Synthia quickly turned toward the voice and became reacquainted with the pleasantly hardened face of Chadric Pearson. His long slender hands held a silver-gilded business card. Synthia pulled back the wind-mussed hair from her eyes as she heard Francis mumble "Gotcha!"

"Sorry, I didn't mean to startle you, Ms. Godbold, just didn't want you to leave without at least trying to see if you might be available for dinner some evening—soon?"

CHAPTER SIXTEEN

Synthia had become so comfortable in Mr. Franklin's office that she did not realize that she had slipped out of her Ferragamos shoes. Something about this man made her feel that the usual social restrictions did not apply in his administrative sanctuary.

Joseph Franklin had returned to the sitting area with two steaming mugs of masala chai. As curious as Synthia was regarding the existence of the secret academy, she could not help but remain even more curious regarding her host. Joseph Franklin seemed so comfortable with himself and the world. As a journalist, Synthia understood that it was not a common trait, regardless of one's station in life.

First of all, she could not physically pinpoint his age. One look gave her the appearance of someone who was enjoying his eighth decade, yet he moved about so easily. Another glance revealed the physique and stamina of someone in his late fifties. She had to find out. Perhaps an indirect approach would work.

"Tell me, Joseph, is there a Mrs. Franklin or are you a jet-setting bachelor?"

"Aren't you a newlywed?" He teased. Synthia blushed.

"I'm only kidding, young lady. Yes, there was definitely a true Mrs. Franklin at one time, Mrs. Ornellia Franklin—my light." Franklin held his large mug in both hands. The steam was still rising, almost dancing in front of Franklin. He continued to look into the undulating vapors as if he might see his Ornellia smiling within. His thoughts opened memory's door. He journeyed to his first meeting with his wife, Ornellia Wortenberry.

CHAPTER **SEVENTEEN**

It was the year 1921. Joseph Franklin was traveling in the rear car of a train bound for Alabama. He was on his way to Coosa, Alabama to visit his cousin and hopefully, to do some carpentry work for a spell. As a boy, Franklin had believed fresh air to be almost synonymous with sawdust. His father, Chike Franklin, had been a master carpenter and was successful in passing the honorable trade down to the quick-learning Joseph.

Franklin got off at his stop in Elmore County and looked around the dusty merchant area which also served as the official train depot. Some passengers hastily made their way to the splintered outhouses that leaned gingerly in the rear area of the makeshift market. Passengers of color made their way to a nearby ditch for their bodily relief.

"Yes, I do believe that I am in Alabama," Franklin said to himself.

A few folks quickly found the water pump, trusting that it was still primed and ready to quench their long held thirst. Once again, the spirit-stripping separation ritual played itself out as America's second-class citizens made their way to the stable area in search of the animal's water trough. Franklin continued to observe the activity until he noticed a small farmer's stand. Long train rides usually meant chewing on hardened bread and jerked meat; items that would last a while on a long journey. Fresh fruit was a welcome and needed treat, providing quick nourishment that immediately invigorated the traveler. Through the years Franklin had learned to appreciate such delicious produce.

Nowadays, a variety of chemicals are added to fruit so it can retain the appearance of freshness. Biting into an apple today gives one the taste of wet cardboard, no matter its color: perception in packaging, deception in product. Franklin remembered the taste of an apple that has been grown by a fastidious farmer. The farmer was one with the soil: he would take early morning walks through his crops, touching and stroking young leaves or budding fruit. There was almost an agreement with the produce: *Mr. Farmer, if you nurture and take care of me, I'll be the most colorful and sweetest fruit there is.*

Biting into a freshly picked apple, one would almost have to hold the remaining fruit up closer to confirm that it was indeed an apple. Had someone unsuspectingly poured honey onto the crimson delicacy?

Spying the plain wooden stand, Franklin's eyes quickly left the tasty offerings to meet the gaze of a young Negro woman who stood behind her freshly picked wares. Ornellia Wortenberry stood at the produce stand with her brother, Buster. She was seventeen years old, and dressed in a plain cotton shift dress. Ornellia was not what many would call pretty, but her hair was neatly braided and she carried a clear dignity. Her lips were full and met imperceptible dimples that lay secreted in her baby-like cheeks.

As Franklin walked closer to the stand, Buster moved a little closer to his sister. Buster had seen Ornellia subtly smooth her dress and move the hair from around her widening chocolate-brown eyes.

"Good day to you," said Franklin. He addressed both but offered no real eye contact to Buster. With a strong baritone voice, Buster spoke first.

"Can I help you?"

"Yes," said Franklin, "I just had a long train ride, and I sure would like some of that fruit. Is there anything good today?" His eyes were still on Ornellia, who blushed at his last comment.

"Everything's good here, mister," said Ornellia. "My brother and me don't sell no bad fruit, that's for the hogs." It didn't get past Franklin that the young woman had quickly established her family relationship with her working partner. Buster was still trying to handle the situation.

"This stuff costs, mister. We ain't given nothing aways."

Okay, Buster, you did your brother thing. I understand, you're supposed to look after your sister, ain't blaming you for that. Now it's time to back off, just a little.

"No, I'm ready to pay for what I eat, how much is it?"

Franklin couldn't rightly recall where he had worked that summer. What he did remember was the fact that he had courted Ornellia and that she had remained by his side for the next sixty-two years. Ornellia was all that Franklin could ask for. She had a stately way of running her household and a never-ending sense of humor. The newlyweds struggled at first but Ornellia would always remind Franklin, "I came from a dirt-poor Alabama town, so we's still be doing all right."

To supplement their income during slow carpentry times, Franklin would do some teaching at one of the local adult sessions at the common schoolhouse or at a church. During the day he would travel about the area, repairing a shed or store shelving here and there. Sometimes he would come home at noon before heading out with his carpentry tools and his writing pads. Franklin's passion was teaching as many people as he could to read. He reminded all who were hesitant that it becomes very difficult for someone to cheat you when there is understanding of a written document.

One day he came home for midday supper. He had left his tools in the front yard area and quietly entered the house. He felt devilish and was going to sneak up on his unsuspecting wife. He heard her moving about in the storage room. Peering around the corner of the entranceway, his eyes met a sight that had never left his memory. Ornellia was clad in a simple off-white sundress. She was ironing dried clothes. She must have been there for a while because one side of the dress had slipped down her left shoulder, granting partial revelation of her creamy-coal breast. Each stroke of the iron gave the same breast a delayed and enticing bounce that threatened to totally escape its cottoned restraint. Next to her was a small bowl of water and starch. Her iron was a hand-me-down one that shamelessly boasted a bent, rusted handle. The iron made its usual home on the edge of an old, sturdy, wooden ironing board. The rays of the midday sun shone strongly through a small window in the room, the rays ending just beyond the basket of clothes. The beam was so bright that Franklin could see the mixture of dust and pollen, gaily swirling within and the steady beam burned as if one could use it as a shelf. It crossed just in front of Ornellia, gently kissing her partially exposed bosom, providing a reflective glow to her dimpled face. Franklin stood there mesmerized by the angelic portrait that was before him. Ornellia continued ironing as she began to sing the first verse of her favorite hymn. Her sweet, husky voice lifted the strains that spoke of her commitment and resolve for patience in this life. "Tempted and tried we're oft make me wonder." By the time she reached the chorus, an audience of birds had assembled in the nearby sycamore tree. They often chirped the afternoon away, but today, they remained silent as Ornellia implored all to "Cheer up my brethren, live in the sunshine. We'll understand it, all by and by."

Franklin dared not beak this wondrous visual reverie. Slowly and carefully, he silently walked backwards, continuing out of the front door. As strange as it was for a man to be sneaking out of his own home, it just didn't feel right to disturb the extraordinary experience that was taking place in the storage room. Ornellia continued until the ironing was done. For years to come, Franklin would wonder how such crisp, ironed clothes could be produced by inferior tools. He would never see any high-tech cleaners match the precision ironing that was done by a poor woman from an Alabama farm.

Franklin worked fifteen-hour days and was tired when he got home. He would take a quick bath and then enjoy a simple, yet delicious meal that his wife set before him. The weariness of the day would be so obvious that Ornellia would not even speak during the meal. Franklin would go to the bedroom and just as the hate and toils of the day attempted to menace his return to mind and spirit, he would slip between Ornellia's freshly ironed sheets. Ornellia's masterful ironing had sealed the heavenly mixture of sunlight, cool breezes, and meadow fragrances that had served to dry the sheets. As soon as Franklin's weight hit the bed, all scents were released, wrapping itself around his fatigued spirit, providing protection from all the world's hurt. Ornellia would crawl in beside him and tenderly stroke him behind the ears. They would soon be in a sound and satisfying sleep. Throughout their years together, Franklin would often recall those simple nights as the most exquisite lovemaking he would ever know.

CHAPTER **EIGHTEEN**

Joseph Franklin set his mug down, wondering how long he had ignored his company with his sojourn into the past.

"Forgive me for leaving you by yourself."

"Huh? I thought that you were just enjoying your tea. I know I am." Synthia sipped her tea.

"Allow me to detain you no further and get to the reason for this pleasant visit."

Synthia actually did not want to end the casual conversation that had made her feel so relaxed. She really wanted to know more about her host. She felt that she needed to ask one more question.

"Joseph, was Ornellia your first wife, your only wife?" He gave her a look that to most might appear as an indication of intrusion into another's private life. To Synthia, it was a look that acknowledged confirmation and revelation. Franklin gave one last look at his mug and posed a question: "Synthia, just what do you know or understand regarding the state of the public school systems in our inner cities?" Synthia looked at Franklin for moment before she responded. At first she wasn't certain if this was the real topic or just a continuation of casual conversation.

"Well, Franklin, my personal feeling is that we are in a state of crisis in regards to the generational outcome of not providing proper education for our children."

"What do you mean?"

"Those children will have children," said Synthia. "Some will achieve success, but the percentages will not change much. And the percentages now suck. I mean the same inner-city issues of poverty, poor health care, and crime will probably continue to exist."

"And what is being done to address this brand new problem?" Synthia laughed. She didn't miss his little joke.

"I'm not totally sure, but there are so many reasons for this tragic problem. Some of the schools have various programs, some work, some don't. I know that there is more money being provided to the schools so that we can level things so to speak."

"Yes. Some schools are getting a good deal of money. It's just too bad that money for schools does not always equal money for the children."

"What?" She almost choked on the tea.

"At times, when money is allocated to a school with the intent on bettering the system... Where does the money wind up? Schools with integrity will allocate to various academic needs, others will find some way to develop several more administrative positions for friendly associates. There is a great personal empowerment in the ability to grant others power. Often intellectual energy and thought is focused on playing the game: the hell with those ungrateful, thuggish, and never-gonna-amount-to-anything kids. I gots mine."

"I don't believe that all administrators are looking to line their pockets."

"Of course they aren't. The problem is how many integrity-challenged educators does it take to constitute a problem? That's all right, dear." He smiled. "Not really looking for an answer. Forgive me for digressing."

"So you're saying that it's a school system problem? That if it wasn't for the few bad teachers or administrators, all would be fine?"

Franklin took a sip of his tea. "Oh, how I wish it were that simple my dear. There is another side of this difficult coin. Our inner-city educational crisis has other important members. I speak, of course, of the missing parent."

"I've heard this argument before, Joseph," said Synthia in a defensive tone. "We can't expect a parent, especially a single mom, to be as available as mothers of the past. We've got to cut them a little slack because many of them are trying to work." She vividly recalled a heated discussion with Taylea and some others at Taylea's hair shop, The Velvet Girl Salon.

CHAPTER NINETEEN

On this humid Saturday, a few months ago, The Velvet Girl Salon was a hotbed for conversation. Discussion topics usually included religion, politics, and family—there was hardly ever any change in individual opinions. On most days, it was exhaustion that announced the conclusion of a particular topic. *Mothers* were the subject of the moment. It was a passionate, hour-long discussion that didn't end until Darrell arrived. He was a shy postal carrier. Of course the ladies of The Velvet Girl Salon never helped Darryl in overcoming his aversion to dialogue. At times, they wouldn't even wait for him to set down the mail before the sultry "Hey, Darrell" or "Bring it over here, Mr. Postman" sounds would travel throughout the room. Even Miss happily-married Taylea would get her catcall in. She often asked Darrell if he had a 'special delivery package' for her today. Somehow the L in delivery would always come with an extra and prolonged tongue movement.

One day Veronica, a middle-aged policewoman, made a comment regarding certain bedroom restraint techniques that she would introduce to Daryl.

"Shush, Veronica," said Nikki, pointing to a lowered hair dryer. "We have a senior church member in the salon today. Let's clean it up everybody!"

"Yes, Veronica," the voice came from under the dryer. "Show a little respect for a mother of the church, will you?" Mrs. Marla Swiftwood pointed an accusatory finger at Veronica and smiled. "Besides, you wouldn't know what to do with that young man. Now me, I'd work him up so bad that he'd be begging for biscuits in the morning. Oh, I'd bake it for him too. Course I'd need some too, just so's I could finish sopping him up!"

"Mrs. Swiftwood." Nikki couldn't believe it. "Just what would your pastor say?"

Mrs. Swiftwood gave her a playful grimace and said, "I didn't say that I wouldn't marry him first." She paused for a moment and lowered her voice. "Course, I wouldn't give him no more than two children—put my foot down on that topic. She hummed an old Sam Cooke tune as she gingerly patted her almost dry hair. For the next few minutes, no hair was being done. The entire salon was fit to be tied.

"Wait a minute, Sister Swiftwood," said Nikki. "What about that nice, elderly gentleman you told us about sometime ago? You know, the one in the park. Y'all never hooked up?"

"Oh, I ain't forgot about him. If I ever see that old charmer again, he's mine. He'd be my meat and potatoes and Darryl my dessert."

"Oh, really?" yelled Taylea from across the salon. "I thought that you said that you were going to be married and all before you shared a bed."

Mrs. Swiftwood looked around the salon, her grinning changing from sheepish to that of a Cheshire cat. "Well, maybe I would have to have a little talk with the pastor on that one. Maybe I could head up an extra bake sale or something. You know, make it up to God."

Taylea threw her hand on her hip and pointed a styling brush at her senior patron. "Ooh, Sister Swiftwood, you going straight to—"

"The Pearly Gates, baby. Straight to the Pearly Gates. Don't you know that there is joy in the Lord? There's gotta be a whole lot of laughter in heaven; God know that I'm only playing. He didn't give us laughter just so we'd have to lock it up." Mrs. Swiftwood again looked around the salon as if she were confirming that no spies were about. "Jesus had all of them disciples, didn't he? Now you gonna tell me that all them twelve men spent all that time hanging out together and nobody had any jokes? Son of God or not, men gonna be men. He came as flesh, didn't he? I know that Jesus probably had some good jokes, especially with all his special powers and such."

"Now, Mrs. Swiftwood," said Taylea, "we ain't got no lightning insurance here, so be careful with God now."

Mrs. Swiftwood dismissed Taylea's playful concern with a wave of her hand. "But alls I'm saying is that every now and then I think on Jesus when he walked on water. Y'all remember that, right? Remember when Peter checked Jesus out and saw him walking on that water? You remember that Peter wanted to do it too. Now Jesus tells him to come on and walk, that he can do it too—the water's fine." She made sure everyone was paying attention.

"So Peter gets all hyped up and begins to walk on the water but then he starts to sink and is soon drinking a whole lot of that water. Now, what if after them other grinning disciples had hauled poor old Peter back into the boat, and Jesus walks over to check on him, that Jesus gets in the boat wearing special made flotation sandals?" The entire shop roared with laughter. One of the departing customers dropped all of her money on the floor. She was so teary-eyed that she couldn't even pick it back up. Mrs. Swiftwood was pleased. She continued. "Could be true. You know, he coulda had it made from goat skin or something. You knows that that boat with them disciples would be almost tipping over cause of the way poor Peter got pranked. Probably, Mark or somebody would mess with Peter and tell him that tomorrow, Jesus was gonna float off of a cliff and what time could Peter be ready?"

With closed eyes, a shrieking Nikki left her station and walked to the front door. She turned to Mrs. Swiftwood and said, "Tomorrow is Sunday—church, front row."

Marla Swiftwood merely grinned and looked toward the ceiling. "Forgive me, Lord, we'll talk later."

CHAPTER TWENTY

"Something funny?" Franklin looked at Synthia. "I'm sorry, my mind just drifted a bit. See what happens when you have a soothing beverage and good company? The mind tends to float away at times. I was just recalling a previous conversation on this matter, kinda."

"It's all right; I'm glad that you're comfortable. I guess that we are both doing a little mind floating this afternoon."

"Let me say this," said a newly focused Synthia, "a lot of parents, especially mothers, have been taking a lot of hits on being available for their children. It's not always their fault."

"No, I don't believe that it's always someone's fault. One thing is certain, however, that someone has to walk to the table and pick up the problem. I know that a parent is not always available, but to remain honest, we have to admit that most can and should play a greater part in their child's academic lives." He glanced at the door thinking that he had heard someone on the other side. He knew that it wasn't Terrence. Perhaps his ears had deceived him: they rarely did. Franklin took another sip of tea and smiled at Synthia. "Sorry, hearing things. Perhaps I really am getting old." He continued with the discussion. "I know that there are more single parents out there than ever before. I also understand that many are struggling, even as they wait to see if dear old dad decides to send money for that particular month. But be it mother, dad or both, somehow we have to become more involved in our children's education." He glanced at the door once more. "Parents just can't make some school functions. Others, we probably convince ourselves that we can't make. My greater concern does not even involve the schools per se. You see, with many of our children, it is obvious that the time was not taken or appreciated regarding his or her discipline. The child was never prepared to be in a structured social environment, let alone one that involves a strong sense of focus." Synthia finished her tea.

She was following her host but just was not sure where this was all going. Franklin sensed her pause. "I say all of this to bring us to the topic at hand." He glanced toward the light-brown package that lay next to Synthia's purse.

She had almost forgotten that she had it with her. *Does he know what's enclosed within the package?*

"Synthia, dear, I believe that we are in agreement that there are many reasons why education in our inner cities has been abysmal for many, many years. We certainly have not even covered some of the more conspiratorial entities that keep this wheel running smoothly—backwards. Be it race, poverty, denial, indifference, or one of my personal favorites, preference, the many spokes are mind-numbing." He studied Synthia. "Within preference is the power of the solution and there is always a solution. How much of modern history must we have missed if we have not observed man's capacity for problem-solving? It is only the solution-shackling power of preference that hinders improvement."

"How can preference stop progress?" said Synthia.

"Let's face it, Synthia, some entities prefer that poor people remain poor and needy. Just like crime is big business, there is big money in needy people. How do you keep folks poor? Simply done, just keep the thunderous weapon of knowledge at bay. Want to really seal the deal, hell, make knowledge the enemy!" Synthia remained silent. "Yes, my dear, the enemy. Offer to support anything that reinforces the personal preferences of the victim. Mismatch the availability of educational resources with, say…that of athletics or shallow entertainment, and one is feeding the perception of preference. The same as with other distractions. If a parent prefers to allow an electronic device to entertain her or his two-year-old, then how prepared is that future student? Oh, all the sassiness and mastery of profanity might be well in place. Some parents deem a child ready for school because he or she has learned to verbally protect herself—an adult preference. From an early age she has been allowed to listen to adult conversations and to be entertained with adult visuals and language. To that child, profanity and attitude are merely normal words and methods of normal communication." He could sense that she was following him. "The tragic humor occurs when the parent exhibits confusion or wonderment when a teacher calls home to complain about the child's classroom language. If the typical parental response was a game show, the host would look at the board and state: 'and the number one answer is—*not my child.*'

"A farmer is rarely in wonderment regarding what he has planted and nurtured. Unless there is unexpected weather or storms in his life, the harvest can be essentially predicted." He watched her gnaw on his words. "That leads me to your discovery, Synthia. Yes, there is a private and very secret academic school that has been teaching since 1977. And yes, raising our young students. People like myself had grown weary of America's de facto policy of what I call 'collateral success'."

"What do you mean by collateral success?" She wished that she had brought along her digital tape recorder.

"Well, the military term of collateral damage refers to a minimal, acceptable level or number of non-military casualties. Casualties are not desired, but in order to win the battle, we will accept this number. Collateral successes, on the other hand, are what I feel to be the acceptable number of successful African-American citizens that some Americans would like to allow. There are vast riches in America's entertainment. 'We'll give you that,' says America.

"America will even allow some successes in areas of business and other professions. But here is also where the rope loses its slack. For some reason, many Americans fear that too many successful people of color will impinge upon the heretofore, limited to some, territories of prosperity. Those on top rarely believe that there is enough for all." He sighed. "New Passage Academy was developed to accelerate the slowly bending curve of collateral success. We are not trying to make a statement regarding who can learn and who cannot learn. We don't care and will not wait until education simultaneously fits into everyone's agenda. What we do know is that, as we wait, lives are perpetually remaining the same." For a moment, the room remained very quiet. Synthia was sitting with her eyes closed, listening to Franklin's every word. She really had not needed for Franklin to inform her that the school did exist. She could tell from his position on education, as well as from his tone, that New Passage Academy was very much real. "Mr. Franklin, Joseph, what is your part in the school. Is it yours?"

"No my dear, it does not belong to me. I am, however, a long-term contributor and occasional overseer of the school. Recently, I have become a bit more active in some of the, shall we say, various arms of the school."

Franklin again glanced in the direction of the door. There was no real audible sound coming from the other side. It was more a subtle sense of something being amiss that distracted the philanthropist. It caused him to remember the sounds of his dog, Sid. Sid had gotten old and weary of this life; Franklin had taken him to the veterinarian to see if anything more could be done for him. The veterinarian had only confirmed Franklin's suspicions and informed that he could perform the solemn task that evening. At first Franklin debated on other possible healing measures. He knew that he could help Sid but understood that good ole Sid's time was done, it was time for his transition. The veterinarian gave Franklin a few private minutes with Sid. When he returned to put Sid down, the warm body of the canine lay in Franklin's lap.

Franklin rose and handed the dog's body to the confused specialist. The doctor knew that the dog's time was eminent, but it was not expected so soon. Yet the dog looked so peaceful the doctor had to stare for a moment to make sure that he was indeed gone.

The sounds at the door somewhat resembled the silent scratching of a lonely dog, but this was very much different. Franklin's eyes were now closed as he sought to see within himself. Synthia saw him give a knowing smile and then he opened his eye to focus on his guest. Synthia gathered herself and leaned forward. She needed to get right to the point.

"Is it true that New Passage Academy actually takes the child from the parents and raises him? Are you telling me that some young mother is strong-armed into losing her child? I understand the city's problems, Mr. Franklin, but I can't condone stripping a child from his mother. I can't."

Franklin allowed her to completely finish. He had often heard this very argument. In fact at times, he welcomed the inquiry. It was almost as if he needed to hear himself defend the academy.

"I do understand, Synthia. Yours is a natural response, as it should be. The removal of a child from the home should be challenged. It is especially vehement when done so by a woman." Synthia immediately gave him a furrowed-brow look.

"Before you accuse me of being patronizing to your gender, let me say this: there is nothing demeaning or minimizing when I speak of a maternal response. I am not implying that you are soft or singularly directed by emotions. We all have emotions; women are freer with theirs, which is an asset, not a liability. To some, emotions imply weakness. Not true. The so-called female 'emotional handicap' is the mighty weapon that has sustained civilization through the centuries. The only reason that it has been labeled as a handicap is because men use it to divert attention from their own developmental shortcomings." Synthia allowed the tension in her shoulders to relax.

"Are you popular with the ladies, Joseph?"

Franklin eased a bit as he noticed that Synthia had returned to using his first name. "Who me? With the ladies? No, I'm just a graying old man."

"Aw, you can't be that old. You seem to get around pretty well, and if not today, you probably were a back-in-the-day catch."

"Hmm, can't even remember my back-in-the-day, young lady." He looked around dramatically for a second. "When God looked around and said 'Let there be light', he sent me to Home Depot for the bulbs."

Synthia threw one of the sofa pillows at her laughing host. She went to take another sip but remembered that the tea was gone.

"More chai?"

"No, I'm fine. But I still need to understand more about this academy."

"Of course."

"Why, or how do you get mothers to give up their child? Just what are you telling them?"

"Let me be very clear: there is absolutely no threatening, coercion or strong-arming of any mother or parent. That is far from our intention. As a matter of fact, many parents absolutely refuse our offer to fully educate and train their child. After all is said and done, there are always plenty who decide that they do want their child to be the beneficiary of a premier education." He paid close attention to her body language. "We don't just offer education, we also focus a great deal of attention on strong character development."

"And do you always produce perfect young men and women?"

"Not at all, nothing's perfect. What we have produced is a profoundly large percentage of success cases. In this world of imperfection, which is preferable?"

"Yes, but it still doesn't negate the fact that you are taking the child from his mother."

"No, what we are doing is merely assisting the mother or parent. You may be a bit too young to remember this, but there was a time, especially in the African-American community, when mothers and fathers would send their child to live with a relative who lived a great distance away. If one were in the south, little Marleen would be placed on a train with a ticket and a name-tag pinned to her lapel. Next stop, New York City. No one would try to promote the area's social preference by making Marleen walk dangerous miles to school there. Perhaps, in that same New York City, another family was putting little Robbie on the train. He's leaving so he could live with big mama in Virginia. Maybe then, he would stop getting in trouble by hanging with the wrong crowd. Yesiree, put 'em on the train. See ya in the summer."

Synthia gave him a quizzical look. "Folks did that, huh?"

"The world was a different place. Sometimes daddy's job might have been seventy miles away. The best he could do was to be home on weekends. Now, between side jobs, mom might also be busy with four or five children. You see, daddy did make up for lost time on Saturdays." Synthia giggled. "Then mom, with her house-cleaning jobs, didn't have but so much time to manage bad little Robbie. So off to big mama's with little Robbie. Didn't always work, but that was the intent. So in essence, you were a family whenever you could be a family. After that, you just survived."

"So, with New Passage Academy, do the parents get to see their children?"

"Yes, they do. The reason we keep it to a minimum, particularly in the beginning, is because we believe that the children may need some social adjusting."

"What?" said Synthia with a sarcastic tone. "You have deprogrammers and such?"

Franklin gave a light laugh. "Oh no, my friend. No programmers, no violence, and no chanting. The human body and mind has a strong capacity to adapt, especially at a young age. As the child adjusts to new circumstances and is bombarded with love within the same environment and positive stimuli, he unknowingly changes as a person. Are you and your husband into sports?"

"We're both football fans. Eagles. We get to a couple of games sometimes."

"Now I know that you are a celebrity, and may not fit this example," said Franklin with a wink, "but I dare you to go to a game and correctly guess the occupations of those seated in the few rows below you. I could give you a sheet with the actual professions and all you would have to do is to match the sixty or so people."

Synthia closed her eyes and received the vision of a typical football game. The brisk, oval stadium would be filled with people wearing all manners of team regalia. Some would have body paint, others homemade hats and elaborate garments. Most would be yelling at the top of their lungs, some even practicing original profanity for the other team or referees. Synthia smiled as she understood Franklin's exercise. During the week, those same high-amplified fanatics might be low-key court attorneys, school librarians or even Darrell, the postal carrier.

"I guess you're saying that most people act differently or conform to the actions of others?"

"And it's been a long time since they were children. Well, at least most of them." He smiled. "I know that it's a rough example, but you understand my meaning. Changed children are the greatest beauty in all of this. The children are essentially given permission to drop their protective guard and merely be children. Once that occurs, something quite glorious happens in which learning is no longer the battle of a teacher trying to cram information into a blocked receptacle. What takes its place is the child becoming what he was all the time: a vessel able and ready to receive information that is now merely poured into a willing host, there—"

Synthia interrupted her host. "I have to see this place, Joseph."

"I believe that is important that you do, Synthia. Terrence will arrange all the necessary travel logistics. I ask you in advance to forgive us for being somewhat covert in our arrangements. Rest assured, you will be more than comfortable with our accommodations."

"I understand and am looking forward to hearing from Terence. Do you have a date in mind?"

"It will be very soon. Let me allow Terrence to exercise his expertise before I commit to a specific day. I can say that it will be within a week. Will that be all right with you?"

"More than all right, Joseph, I'm looking forward to it."

"Then it's settled, New Passage Academy awaits you."

CHAPTER **TWENTY-ONE**

Buildings that once breathed with the activity of families and businesses now stood as dull brick skeletons. The entire neighborhood had been relocated; the structures were slated for demolition, soon to be replaced by high-end condominiums. The air was filled with the pungent odor of unfiltered diesel fuel that belched from a variety of construction equipment. Crazy George, the back-hoe operator, performed what he thought would be his last mechanical plunge into the pebbled earth. He felt a quick shudder from his cab as the motor once again strained to remain running, but with a last piston-driven gasp, turned silent.

"Damn this cheap piece of American don't-really-know-how!" This was the third time in two days his engine had failed him and, despite complaints to the foreman, no one seemed interested in replacing the relatively new unit. The only intervention had been from a dour mechanic who had replaced a few hoses, turned a few bolts, and with a grunt, declared it fit for battle. I knows they got the money, thought Crazy George, *somebody probably behind on some payola that's all. Let some politician do his meet-the-press walkabout and betcha stuff start working right.*

He tried one more time to coax the engine, but nothing happened. "I give up!" George heaved his tired frame from the crippled metal hulk. "Somebody's just gonna hav'ta get off some money and buy a decent hoe," he said, smiling at the barroom joke as he strode past the fresh mound of hard soil.

"What the...?" Crazy George almost tripped. He looked down and noticed that something had almost snagged itself on his ankle. If he didn't know any better, he could swear that it briefly wrapped itself around his ankle to trip him. Believing it was a branch of some sort, George turned to give it a satisfying kick when he stopped in midswing. This was no branch. What George saw was a human bone, a dusty, gray hand and splintered forearm that lay open in the afternoon sun. Forgetting to blink, Crazy

George stared at the partial skeleton then gathered himself as he reached toward the grisly discovery. His hand touched something sharp as he set his muddied water jug on the newly turned earth. With his senses heightened, he jerked around and found himself confronted with other earth-toned skeletal pieces that protruded from the mound as if vainly seeking restoration via the sun's warming rays. Crazy or not, all George could now do was bolt toward the foreman's trailer with the story of his unusual find. What he did not realize was that his discovery would trigger an extraordinary chain of events.

The weary stranger sat alone, ignoring the various activities of the park. He remained focused on two women who were in an animated conversation. They were initially too far away to enable a reasonable view of their unsuspecting faces. The iron and wooden park bench had given him a lovely combination of sun and shade. Still, he had to get closer to the ladies—especially the pretty news lady.

Squeezing a better grip on his cane, the stranger both pushed and pulled himself up to his feet. In a circular fashion he ambled toward a better bench for observation. Wincing from a fleeting pain in his chest, he closed his eyes to will the pain away. He often cursed a body that continued to betray its owner. In years past he had been able to ignore the nuisance bodily distractions that reminded him of man's limited earthly time. Years of hard work, coupled with the bulging pains of the soul, had continued to exact a cost that declared a piece of sculptured wood as his life partner. However, the stranger was an infrequent visitor to self-pity parties. Life was what it was. His had been generous in its dispensation of woe, but he understood that others would fight to have only his trials. What angered the stranger was the fact that life now placed him in the category of the stalkers that he had often read about. He never thought that this would be his story. *Hell, we all think that we know our full stories. We think that we can predict what we would do and what we wouldn't do. Ain't nobody ever been that smart. Keep living, life will change your song.*

He remembered the words of his mother. Life had now compelled him to monitor the steps of an innocent woman. It wasn't easy with his challenged health. At times he had lost sight of her and had to abandon his objective for the day. He knew the address of her and her husband's home. He had seen them both leave their expensive building, wondering how much it cost. He just had to get close to do what needed to be done. It didn't matter how tired he was, some things just needed to happen. It was as if a voice was speaking to him, informing him that time was of the essence, informing him that matters had to be quickly settled. The stranger had learned not to ignore certain whisperings.

He turned his attention back toward the women. They seemed to be enjoying their ice cream cones. It was time to have a face-to-face encounter.

CHAPTER **TWENTY-TWO**

Synthia and Taylea completed their power walk and ice cream expedition. They were spooning their peanut brittle and rocky road respectively, and had secured their usual, comfortable perch near the playground area where a few young mothers stood sentry to a high-pitched swarm of children.

"Glad we could finally hook up, Synthia," said Taylea.

"We haven't gotten together for our exercise in a good while." She made a finger-quoting gesture. They both looked at their ice cream and laughed.

"Yes, you're right, Taylea. I do miss this and I miss you."

"What you also need to do is to stop by the salon more often. What is it, got somebody else doing your hair now?" Taylea lowered her head, giving her dairy partner a pseudo-serious look. "Now, what did I tell you about getting famous and then leaving us for uppity pastures?"

Synthia remembered Taylea's teasing regarding the propensity of those who become successful to forget those who had assisted them when fame was still a long distant maybe.

"No, Miss Taylea of The Velvet Girl Salon and the Perpetual-Advice-Institute, even-if-it's-mostly-her-opinion, Inc."

"Oh, been working on that one a while, have we?" Taylea laughed.

"Relax, Lady T., you're still my queen of the ebony coiffs."

"That's *all* coiffs, my sister, just so's you know."

"And I do, my bad."

They didn't notice the stranger who half-stood, half-leaned on the rear corner of the park bench.

"Excuse me, ma'am."

Initially startled, both Taylea and Synthia looked at the stranger. He side-stepped the bench and now stood directly in front of them. He was modest in height, his frame cautiously sturdy. He wore a slightly crumpled, newsboy-type cap that was reminiscent of a blue-collar worker of the 1940s. He leaned slightly to the right, supported by a well-traveled cane. They thought it odd that they had not seen the man as he approached.

Taylea's defenses went up. "Can we help you with something?"

For a moment the stranger didn't speak. He just studied Synthia's face. When he was satisfied, he responded to Taylea: "Please forgive my intrusion, ladies," he said, tipping his cap. "I don't mean any harm, just want to ask a question." Synthia assessed his face, trying to confirm friendliness or hostility. His face told of one who had toiled hard and long through the years. Perhaps his most meaning reward was his need for the cane. Was he here for a handout? Somehow Synthia didn't think so. There was something, some familiarity in his unwavering eyes that made her return his stare. What was it?

"What question do you have, sir?" said Taylea. "Are you looking for directions or money?"

"No, don't need any money, ma'am. As for directions, I'm pretty certain of where I'm going." Something in his last response did not sit well with Synthia. He didn't as much say the words as much as he sighed them.

"What can we do for you today, sir?" said Synthia.

"I merely wanted to know if you were Synthia Pearson, the newlywed reporter?"

"Yes, she's Mrs. Godbold-Pearson," said Taylea. "You looking for a job, need an autograph?"

"Don't need anything." He extended his hand to Synthia. "I just wanted to personally meet such a fine woman and wish her a long and prosperous marriage. You do make each other happy?"

Synthia took his hand, taking one more glance at his eyes. "Well, thank you for those well wishes. You have a safe day. I'm sorry, I didn't get your name, sir."

He held her hand, not roughly, but seemingly unable to release his grip. His head dropped slightly, angling toward the left. His eyes glanced upward as if he were listening to someone who was not physically present.

It was Taylea who broke the moment. She took his hand away from Synthia's, replacing it with hers. "My name is Taylea, Taylea Roland. We're just sitting here waiting for our husbands to come back from the hot-dog stand."

"Pleased to meet you, Taylea. Forgive me, I don't mean to come off as weird, though I know that I do." He chanced one more look at Synthia and then tipped his cap to both the women. "I've disturbed you long enough. I shall be on my way." He turned to Synthia. "My name doesn't matter, hasn't for a long time now. I am, however, very pleased to have made your acquaintance. Please do not think ill of this intruding old man. Have a long and blessed life together."

Taylea remained silent. Something about the gentleman was intriguing. With her 'people antennae' now raised, she actually wanted to speak further with this stranger whose name did not matter. Synthia and Taylea watched the leaning man steadily make his way toward the shaded area of the park. Taylea looked at her friend.

"What was that all about?"

"You know, I'm still not very sure. I really could not read him. Part of me wanted to get information, the other part was looking for park security."

"What, when he wouldn't let go of your hand?"

"No, not really. It wasn't that he had me in a strong grip or anything. It was almost like he was trying to communicate with me through touch."

"Oh God, now you're saying that he was an alien who was trying to capture your spirit and replace it with one of his friends from the mother ship." Taylea did a quick scan of the sky for added effect. "Swing down and let me ride, 'cause she don't want to go," she said, pointing at Synthia.

"Ha ha, Star Child jokes. Actually, for a moment there, I thought that you were cheating on Roland and your sugar daddy was introducing himself to me."

"Yeah, you know how I like it. Ain't nothing like senior citizen love. He probably keeps his Viagra in that hollowed-out cane. Now if his cane is like—"

"There are children here, Taylea!"

"Like they ain't seen Viagra commercials? Please, girl, these kids see more by the age of two than we saw at seventeen!"

The laughter failed to erase the mystery of the past few minutes. Something still troubled Synthia regarding the man's presence. Their conversation moved on from a debate regarding a second serving of ice cream to an upcoming jazz music festival. Taylea gave Synthia a few squinting looks as she lamented the decreasing art of good stage presence in many of the current acts. Their conversation ceased as they took some time to take in the other activities of the park. In unison they tilted their heads back to fully appreciate a serpentine breeze that eased throughout the park. They both had their eyes closed when Synthia spoke. "Taylea?"

"Oh, you're finally gonna tell me what's on your mind?"

"Didn't think that it was that obvious."

"Oh, it wasn't. Taylea just knows."

"I do seem to forget that you have those marvelous skills."

"Enough about me, unless you're finished of course. What's been bothering you?"

Synthia gave her friend a playful push. It pleased her how Taylea could ostentatiously love herself and still not be offensive to anyone.

"I'm sure that you've heard about the rumors regarding the secret, private school for inner-city children."

"Yeah, honey, I've picked up a few notes on the wind. Can't own a beauty salon and not get a touch of the grapevine here and there. Is this a personal or professional inquiry?" This was not the first time that Synthia had used Taylea to vent her thoughts. Although it appeared a paradox, the proprietor of a beauty salon could always be trusted when issues were presented as private matters. Officially, Synthia couldn't speak of work-related issues. Even Chadric respected the boundaries of confidentiality and would allow her distance. Taylea poked fun at herself and was often the first and last to be heard; but she possessed a wisdom that spoke of silver-haired nurturers of days gone by. Her senses and thoughts knew when to listen to the breathing, as well as the words. There were times when all Synthia really required was to voice out loud some of things that were troubling her. Taylea even appeared to know when a response was not required. She would patiently listen, give a moment of pause, and then ask Synthia what she thought of the latest topic on *The View.* Synthia would return home feeling much better that she had gotten the chance to "talk it out" and receive good advice from her friend.

"This is one of those times when the problem is both business and personal," said Synthia."

"Now you really have me," said Taylea, shooing an approaching pigeon. Synthia paused for a moment. She did not want to divulge too much to Taylea: this was indeed an explosive issue and should be handled with care.

"Well, just let me ask it this way: if the rumors were true, and there existed a school that educates our children in secret, where would you stand? Before you answer that, also consider a requirement that the parents have very limited access to their children. In fact, the school actually raises the child. Who's right?"

Taylea looked at her friend for a moment. She had heard the current gossip and had privately mused regarding its merit. Surprisingly, a usually opinionated Taylea was still caught in a social conundrum.

"To be very honest with you, Synthia, this problem really had me in unfamiliar territory, perched on the fence. My immediate thoughts were, hell, why not? I'll take the lesser of two imperfections, you know? But then, other thoughts came to mind such as, why does it have to be this way? Can't that same money and know-how be used within our cities? What about the psychological issues with the children? After a few years, who are the children emotionally attached to? Who is watching over the spiritual well-being of the school, or is religion not encouraged?" She watched a group of pigeons land nearby. "You see, Synthia, there are many issues that defines who one is. Now just what God committee is making these decisions?"

Synthia gave her friend a serious look. "My, you have thought on this matter, haven't you? Want a job at the station as an analyst?"

Taylea studied her nails, then slowly turned to her park buddy.

"Who me? I'm just a little ghetto beauty-shop owner."

"Seriously though," said Synthia, "I didn't look at it in that manner. Yes, there are many issues that do come to play in this drama."

"Speaking of drama, is this a big time story for our famous star reporter? No, I don't want you to answer that. I just wanted to see your face. I don't mean that in a nosey way. I can see that it's not messing with your mind as much as it is with your spirit." She nudged Synthia. "Now we've had enough salon conversations for me to know where you stand on school and violence issues. Hell, the newspapers could save a lot of money by just preprinting the report of a murder or drive-by and leaving the names blank. All they need to give folks is a list of names and a date, tell us to fill it in for the day. Girl, I know you got pain. All I got to do is read it, you have to report it." This time she touched her hand. "One thing I believe in, Synthia, is in you trusting your heart. This story is probably gonna take you places that you'd rather not be. It's okay, your heart has been leading you this far. Ain't a perfect compass, just your best one."

Synthia smiled as she allowed her head to lean back to meet another adventurous breeze. Her friend never failed her.

"Mmm, speaking of schools, I'd like to take him home and be his tutor for a year or so."

Huh? thought Synthia. She lowered her head and looked at her distracted friend. Two men were riding along the bicycle path, one in green, the other in purple. Their speed was not great, but one could tell that they had been at it for a while. Their sinewy leg muscles moved in perfected piston-like syncopation, propelling their high-end cycles in unison with the wind. One of the cyclists broke stride to get a drink of water, the stream of liquid meeting both mouth and chest.

"Ooh, that one's mine!" screamed Taylea.

"Taylea, they can hear you," whispered Synthia as she grabbed her arm.

"They're supposed to hear, girl. Think I care? Oh, you don't want one? I'll take'em both! Y'all do your thing," she yelled at the bikers. "Three's better than two!" She licked her lips. The two riders turned toward Taylea and gave her a friendly it's-all-in-good-fun wave. "Where's Johnny Gill when you need him?" said Taylea; "My, my, my!"

"Forgetting your wedding ring, Mrs. Snead?"

"Synthia, you just have to learn to lighten up. It's all in good fun. Ain't nobody trying to do nothing. I laugh, they laugh. You think if Roland was here that I'd be quiet?" Synthia had to admit that Taylea had her on that one. She'd still be making cracks with her husband Roland right beside her. If Roland possessed an ounce of fat, he kept it in a safe deposit box. The ex-con, now college student, did not prance about in a tight-fitting shirt and would not have made some bravado-like gesture toward the bikers. Knowing and loving his playful wife, he'd probably have just gotten up and given the bikers a smiling what-can-I-do shrug and made his way to the concession stand.

"I'm sorry, Taylea. I can't even enjoy a fun moment without being all dark and dreary."

"It's all right, Mrs. Allen Poe. They're coming back this way anyway."

Synthia's widened eyes leaped toward the bicycle path.

"Gotcha! Now the only question you have to answer is did I get all big-eyed because I was scared that they were coming to see us, or was it because you were hoping that they were coming to see us? Ooh, don't answer that, we'll now have a word from our sponsor."

CHAPTER TWENTY-THREE

The simple, teal-colored ranch home sat in the middle of a suburban neighborhood. The homes were threatening to resemble the broken-down city blocks from which many of the residents had previously escaped. One could tell that the neighborhood was once beautiful but owner neglect had slowly taken its negative hold on the area's property value. True, many residents still fought the good fight. They continued to maintain driveways, repair windows, and keep fading lawns trimmed. A changing economy, along with the closure of some of the area's businesses, had spawned a ripple effect of decreased incomes, increased financial arguments, and occasional household separations.

Outside the house Reverend Sydney, Deaconess Pennywell, and Sister Tatum sat in the reverend's dark-blue Lincoln Town Car. They were, once again, reviewing their strategies for their meeting with Sister Snowden. Having reconfirmed their diplomatic approach, the church members proceeded to the front door. Before knocking, the door swung open.

Sister Quentella Snowden stood there with her hands on her hips. She had been watching from the window and wondering why the pastor had remained in the car. Reverend Sydney had called beforehand to request a brief visit, ensuring her that as a Christian gentleman, he would also have two of the church sisters with him. Reverend Sydney repeated to Sister Snowden that it was a somewhat personal, but not urgent matter.

"Welcome, reverend, it is good to see you and the sisters here. Please come right in."

"And good evening to you, Sister Snowden," said the reverend. "I do appreciate you seeing us on such short notice."

"I must admit, I am a bit confused, but please, let's sit down, shall we?"

"I realize that we're taking up your time, Sister Snowden, so I'll get right to the point. It's regarding your friend, Mr. Fellyard Beedley."

"Mr. Beedley? Why… is there is a problem? Is he okay? Did something happen?"

"Oh no, nothing like that, Sister Snowden. What we'd like to understand better is how Mr. Beedley has been treating you. I mean that he, at times, presents himself as being, let's say, detached from normal actions. In our concern we want to make sure that he is not hiding something that may eventually cause you harm."

"Hiding something? I don't understand," said Sister Snowden.

Sister Tatum decided to jump in and help the pastor out. "What the reverend is trying to say, dear sister, is that there has been some talk around the neighborhood regarding Mr. Beedley, and let us say, some of his strange habits."

"Habits, what type of habits? I still don't understand." Sister Snowden leaned back in her chair.

"Well, for one," said Deaconess Pennywell, "he is rarely seen during the daytime. And when he is seen, he always seem to be lurking about, never engaging with anyone. It's not that he's impolite, just not friendly."

"And that's why you all are here, because someone doesn't appear friendly?" She looked at each of them. "This is why you all got together, to come tell me this?"

"No, it's not quite that simple, dear sister," said the reverend. He glanced toward his associates. "We are not here to tell you what to do or how to do it. I am your reverend only. I'm not pretending to be your father, but I am concerned. We all know how this world has changed and that there are some characters out there who prey on the elderly. It could be contractors, or it might be unscrupulous salesmen who are looking for a little easy money. They all understand that many older folk, although not rich, do have some disposable income." He looked at the other sisters for support. "We just want to make sure that he has not made any type of inquires that deal with, maybe your money, or any legal documents. Not saying that you can be easily tricked, we're just concerned for one of our own, our precious own." Everyone was quiet, thinking.

"You see," said Reverend Sydney, "the way he acts, where he is seen—or not seen for that matter—might make one unsure of his mindset. Sister Snowden, even some of his yard furniture possesses a very disconcerting look to them, evil if you will. I will be honest with you, it is nothing I can put my finger on. It's a matter of bits and pieces telling the bigger story: alone the pieces seem relatively harmless." The reverend leaned forward to touch Sister Snowden's hand. "Please understand, we just want to make sure that everything is okay with you. We are not so wrapped up in the church that we don't understand worldly affairs."

Sister Snowden's voice raised an octave. "Affairs? Who said anything about an affair?" she asked.

"Oh no, sister, I'm speaking of happenings in the world. I would never accuse you of anything like that! What I'm trying to say is, and I'm not saying that this is the case, but some men or women have tried to seize the opportunity to gain something when associating with someone who resides alone."

Sister Snowden pulled her hand away. "So you're telling me that I'm too feeble in the mind to understand if someone's trying to fool me. You telling me that if a man finds an interest in me that it has to be something other than my character or personality. Is this what you're saying? I, too, have been around a good while. Now, reverend, sisters, I think I know when someone's trying to manipulate me. Perhaps a little like… right now."

Deaconess Pennywell spoke up. "Why don't we all pause for just a second? Perhaps we can get a better understanding of all of this. Now I know how this looks, Sister Snowden. Someone intrudes in your own home, having the gall to try to inform you about a special friend. Anyone's natural reaction is to take offense, that's human. Try to understand this: no one sat around just trying to decide how we can get in Sister Snowden's business and mess up her evening."

Sister Snowden sat with a hardened look as Deaconess Pennywell continued. "If we are about what we're supposed to be about, that is, being a church family and all, we're supposed to look out for one another. Maybe we're just saying it all wrong and if so, forgive us. But we do care. The main thing here is this: we do love you and care about you. We do understand that you're a grown woman with a right to her own business without any meddling. But please, we show no love if we think that something may be slightly amiss and we do nothing. I'm not saying that it would happen, but how hurt would we all be if something did happen and we all just looked at each other, wishing that we had spoken to you?" Sister Snowden relaxed a bit, her breathing subsided and her jaws became less taut. Still, she was not completely forgiving toward her guests. Her eyes moved to each visitor. "I do believe that you came here with good intentions, but still, it's a very personal and hurtful intrusion."

"Let's just call it what it is," said Reverend Sydney, "it is an intrusion, but an intrusion in the best light. We just don't want anything to happen to you, my sister, and if this man is just visiting with you and is treating you right, then we certainly have no problems: end of discussion. But again, there are certain things about this man that suggests that all is not well. We just don't want that touching you. Nevertheless, we've taken up enough for your time. I pray that you do not think too ill of us and that our relationship has not been drastically challenged."

Sister Snowden stood up. A small smile of understanding attempted to make its way to her face. "No, Reverend Sydney, sisters, I don't think ill of you. I just know that Mr. Beedley has been nothing but a gentleman. All we've ever done is to share some dinner and some fine conversation with each other. He has never inquired about my finances or even the value of my home."

"Then my sister," said the reverend, "may I wish you nothing but continued good dinners and fine discussions. Sisters, allow me to take you home. Thank you again, Sister Snowden." They exchanged hugs and made their way to the door.

As Sister Snowden opened the door, she turned toward the reverend and said, "Is Sister Synthia Pearson still a member of our church? I haven't seen her in a while."

"To my knowledge she remains a member in good standing. Her job does take her in many directions. And of course, she's still essentially a newlywed. I'm sure there are some different household issues that need to be addressed regarding her and her husband's places of worship and all that."

"Like you said, reverend," said Sister Tatum, "they are still newlyweds. She may not have been at church, but I'm sure the name Jesus has been mentioned a couple of times."

"Sister Tatum!" said Deaconess Pennywell. "The reverend's right here!"

"You're quite right, Deaconess Pennywell. He's right here on Earth, he understands." Reverend Sydney smiled and rolled his eyes and shook his head a couple times.

"I'm sorry; you were saying, Sister Snowden?"

"It's just that Mr. Beedley was inquiring about Sister Synthia. He wanted to know was she still involved at church, if she had any close friends there."

Sister Tatum did a quick turn on the steps. "Why? Is he a friend or relative of Sister Synthia?"

Reverend Sydney said. "I don't remember seeing him at the wedding." Reverend Sydney paused. His memory was challenging what he was saying. He hadn't seen him, had he? The confusion in memory usually wouldn't bother him, but for some reason this didn't fall under the memory relapse category. This caused a slight disturbance in his very spirit.

"You know something, reverend, perhaps you and the sisters could find an opportunity to just meet Mr. Beedley. Then you'd understand that all is well. I believe he's home this evening. Let me call him, all right? Maybe he can see you tonight."

Reverend Sydney was a bold man for Christ, but still he said, "Right now?" He was not feeling quite strong enough for a meeting with Mr. Fellyard Beedley.

On the other hand, Sister Tatum was immediately interested regarding the possibility to meet the *boyfriend* of Sister Snowden. "Yes, yes, that's a good idea, Sister Snowden. Go ahead and call and see if he's home. Tell him that your church family is making neighborly visits and would like an opportunity to say hello, welcome him to the church community and all." Reverend Sydney's hands were tied. He knew he had to go. He just hoped that the number Sister Snowden was dialing would not be answered.

"Yes, they're right here," said Sister Snowden into the receiver. "They'd love to stop by and visit…just for a few minutes. I've told them so much about you." She looked up at Reverend Sydney and nodded. "They'll be right over." For a moment Reverend Sydney thought his heart had skipped a much needed beat.

They bid farewell to Sister Snowden and walked to the car. Deaconess Pennywell had Fellyard Beedley's home address in hand, although it was not needed. Reverend Sydney knew the house.

The sun was now completely set. The sky welcomed a new night. Reverend Sydney, Deaconess Pennywell, and Sister Tatum sat in the reverend's automobile. They sat in front of the home of Fellyard Beedley, Sister Snowden's new friend. This time no one was speaking. They all were mentally rehearsing their respective lines of conversation. Deaconess Pennywell was pensive, her posture rigid. Reverend Sydney opened the car doors.

"Let's get it over with." He started up the driveway.

"Coming, my sister?" said Sister Tatum, looking over her shoulder at Deaconess Pennywell, who was still in the car. There was no answer. Reverend Sydney walked back to the car and held the door slightly ajar.

"Are you okay, deaconess?" Deaconess Pennywell didn't speak. Some of the color had faded from her face. She finally looked up at Reverend Sydney.

"I don't think I really want to meet him, meet Mr. Beedley. I just can't go in there." She slowly turned away from Reverend Sydney's gaze. Part of the Reverend Sydney wanted to ask the Deaconess to slide over so he could join her in the car. They could both wait and allow the overly curious Sister Tatum to handle the interview. *C'mon, he thought, you were called to be a leader for good times and bad. Time to go to work.*

Sister Tatum was confused. She looked at Reverend Sydney as he joined her on the walkway. He gave Sister Tatum a let's-not-talk-about-it-now gesture. They made their way up the walkway.

"Is she okay?" whispered Sister Tatum.

"She'll be fine."

CHAPTER TWENTY-FOUR

Fellyard's home was a simple structure, well-lit and pleasing to the eye. A neatness defined the dwelling. There were no rusted gates or broken-down shutters. What did bother Reverend Sydney was the oddity in the front yard. The arrangement was neither crude nor obscene, but a weird collection of three wooden orbs and oddly angled four-by-fours. It was the manner in which they were distributed throughout the lawn that didn't sit well with Reverend Sydney. He just could not put his finger on it but it almost reminded him of something created by a bygone civilization. A quick glance would give passersby no cause to think that anything was amiss. For the most part, observations were concluded with a thought of *that's interesting.*

The doorbell was very modern, almost cheerful sounding. Reverend Sydney and Sister Tatum stood at the door waiting for someone to answer. Even Sister Tatum now wished that no one would answer. Finally the door opened and Fellyard Beedley addressed his visitors. He wore coveralls that covered a slight and sinewy frame, which immediately reminded one of a farmer from some Midwestern patch of land. In fact, brought to mind the elder Pa Joad in Steinbeck's *Grapes of Wrath.* Fellyard Beedley looked at his two guests for a moment. He held Reverend Sydney's eyes.

"Please, do come in. Is it just the two of you? Where is the good deaconess?"

"She's not feeling her best right now," said Reverend Sydney. *Forgive me, Lord,* he thought.

"Well, perhaps it is best if she does rest in the car right now."

Reverend Sydney had a puzzled look. *I guess he could see us out of the window. But if he could see us, why did it take so long to answer the door?*

"You say something, Reverend Sydney?" said Mr. Beedley. "Please come in and have a seat."

The reverend and Sister Tatum followed Fellyard Beedley into his living room area. The house was clean. The furniture simple, yet quite comfortable. *Perhaps we made an error,* thought Reverend Sydney. *All is probably well.*

"You have to excuse me, reverend," said Fellyard. "I don't get the chance to entertain much, but I'm so glad that you could come. Can I get you two anything, a warm toddy perhaps?"

"Actually, we don't want to take up too much of your time, Mr. Beedley."

"Please, call me Fellyard, or even just Beedley. Doesn't matter. I answer to both. I've actually answered to many names."

He gave an odd grin and seated himself on a wooden rocker. The pause in conversation gave Sister Tatum time to take a more thorough observation of the home. There was something that was out of place. For a moment it confused her and then it registered: no pictures. There were no landscapes or baubles, not even the obligatory old family portrait. Although clean, the papered walls were essentially bare. What was present was a small statue that stood poised on the floor in the far corner of the room. It stood about two feet high and was the full-figure of a man, carved from darkened wood. Its facial features were difficult to discern from a distance. The man's back was hunched; the head was oddly angled to the side. The arms were extended out, its left hand clenched. Sister Tatum wasn't sure, but it appeared that something was near its feet. There was the subtle scent of pine cleaner in the air. Sister Tatum's practiced nose reminded her that it was the smell that was usually appreciated on a Saturday morning, right after a good cleaning.

Well, maybe Mr. Beedley, expecting our visit, did a quick clean-up, thought Sister Tatum. The pine oil smell did not seem to be a byproduct of cleaning. Why was she feeling a sense of something being masked?

The living room was well illuminated by three matching lamps. Reverend Sydney appreciated each sharply lit lamp.

Beautiful lamps, he thought, nice and bright. It was almost as if each bulb were new, that they had patiently waited for a chance to show what they could do. Both Reverend Sydney and Sister Tatum sat on the edge of the quilt-covered couch. They were both subconsciously minimizing their contact with the furniture, avoiding the feeling of being stained.

"You're sure that I can't get you something from the kitchen? I feel like such a poor host."

"No, we are fine, thank you very much," said Reverend Sydney. "Like we stated before, we won't be here long. We apologize for intruding upon you with a last minute call. We were already at Sister Snowden's and didn't want to miss the opportunity to meet you. If we keep waiting, next thing we know it would be four months later and we'd still be without introductions."

Reverend Sydney offered Fellyard his hand again. "First and foremost, let me welcome you to the neighborhood, and also extend you an invitation to stop by the Church when your time permits, of course."

"Why I would love to visit your fine church. It's just that my days are usually so tied up."

"Do you work?" said Sister Tatum. She was not shy.

"No, my dear, I am very much retired. For the most part I am involved in, shall we say…worldly affairs." He gave Reverend Sydney an odd smirk as if they were sharing an inside joke.

"Active in what way, Mr. Beedley?" said Sister Tatum. "Do you volunteer, or is this a paid vocation?"

"Yes," said Fellyard.

Both Sister Tatum and Reverend Sydney looked at each other regarding the ambiguous answer. Sister Tatum was confused. She allowed her gaze to return to the room's lack of décor. A cry almost escaped from her lips as she glanced toward the statue that stood with two clenched fists. She struggled to rationalize her thoughts. Surely she had to be mistaken in her previous survey of the statue. Something inside of her refused to allow her that peace. She lowered her head for private communion.

"Mr. Beedley," said Reverend Sydney, "I'm going to be polite but respectfully blunt." He leaned on the arm of the couch. "We did stop by the home of Sister Snowden because we are concerned about her association with you. It is not that we have anything against you and all; it's just that we really don't know you, hadn't really seen you. We want to make sure that all was well with our dear Sister Snowden. You understand this, of course."

Fellyard's face offered a small smile toward his guests. "Yes, I do understand, good reverend. I've long been a man of this world, and I understand the need for concern. I also understand that one must protect his own. I am not unmindful that there are those out there who conspire against many of our fine, older citizens..." His voice trailed off. "Let me reassure you, I have no intention other than to share friendly dinners and polite conversations with Mrs. Snowden. She's a gracious host and an interesting companion. Let me also state that I am a man of means, humble means, but means just the same. I have no ill intentions, financial or otherwise regarding Mrs. Snowden."

"I appreciate and thank you for your honesty as well as your understanding," said Reverend Sydney. "Again, it's not a personal slight against you, just a matter of everyone's appreciation of this darker world. We are very happy for our Sister Snowden. If she has found good companionship, then all is more than fine. We just wanted to do our Christian duty."

Fellyard waved a dismissive hand. "Think nothing of it, reverend. I apologize for not introducing myself to you earlier. I should have taken the time to stop by the church to meet you." He turned toward Sister Tatum. "And to you as well, Mrs. Tatum." His comment reminded Reverend Sydney of something Sister Snowden had mentioned.

"Mr. Beedley, are you a friend or a relative of Synthia Pearson?" Fellyard's body remained passive, but his eyes momentarily betrayed his malevolent feeling toward the news reporter. He quickly recovered. "Oh, why do you ask, reverend?"

"It's just that I'm not certain if I saw you at her wedding awhile back. Thought that maybe you might even be associated with her husband Chadric." Fellyard's immediate thought was to say no. He knew that, for the most part, he functioned on life's fringes and therefore it would be easy to confuse someone into thinking that he was or was not somewhere. For some reason he didn't feel that he could fool Reverend Sydney. Besides, Fellyard's mind had quickly processed the probability that his friend, Mrs. Snowden, might have mentioned his inquiry regarding Mrs. Pearson.

"No, I'm sorry to say that I don't know any of those fine people. I have, however, been trying to meet Mrs. Pearson. She's a journalist, and I have some very old artifacts that might make an excellent feature story for her television station."

"Well, I don't know if she does those types of things anymore," said Sister Tatum. "Why don't you just call the station?"

"That's probably the best way to handle these things," said Fellyard. "Thank you, Mrs. Tatum, I'll do just that." He moved closer to Sister Tatum, his eyes focused on her chest. Sister Tatum's left hand reflexively moved to her breast.

"What an interesting brooch you're wearing, Mrs. Tatum. Where did you get it?" He admired her breast.

"It's something that was handed down to me from my mother," said Sister Tatum. "It's one of those family heirlooms, passed down from daughter to daughter."

Fellyard's hairy fingers touched the brooch. "Yes, I do know. It is very interesting as well as very beautiful. This particular piece is very similar to the ones worn during the days of slavery. At the time it was worn as a necklace by some of the older slave women on the plantations. Its intricate pattern had a meaning that was related to them returning home."

"Oh, are you a historian?" said Reverend Sydney.

"Dear reverend, you cannot imagine how I feel about walking through history." Sister Tatum's personal code was that a man's fingers should not be on her person, let alone her bosom. She would not let him linger.

Reverend Sydney stepped in. "I guess we've taken too much of your time, Mr. Beedley. Again, our apologies if we have offended you. However, I'm not doing my job if I'm not looking after my flock. It's a shepherd thing, you know?"

"Oh yes, a shepherd thing. I am very familiar with the shepherd thing, my good reverend." Reverend Sydney had to ask just one more time.

"You're certain that we haven't met before? I don't know why, but I'm feeling like I should know you."

"No, I'm sorry that I have not had the pleasure before tonight. Perhaps I just have one of those faces."

You certainly don't have one of those faces, thought Sister Tatum. That face would not be confused with any other.

"I again apologize for the late and surprise visit," said Reverend Sydney. "You have been gracious."

"Think nothing of it, reverend. Please come again when we can enjoy a longer visit. Maybe next time I will have the pleasure of formally meeting Deaconess Pennywell."

Reverend Sydney's mouth opened a bit wider as he realized that he had forgotten about Deaconess Pennywell, who remained in the car.

"Perhaps we should hasten, Sister Tatum," said Reverend Sydney. There was no answer. Sister Tatum was already making her way down the walkway.

CHAPTER **TWENTY-FIVE**

It was 7:30 when the telephone in Synthia's hotel room interrupted the morning's stillness.

"Hello," she said, fighting off a long sleep.

"The shuttle will be in front of the hotel at 9:45am," said a pleasant voice. Three days prior, Synthia had been informed by Terrence that she had a flight scheduled on one of the consortium's private jets. Her flight would take off from Philadelphia airport for a quick hop to Maryland. Her flight had been slightly delayed by runway traffic; therefore, after checking in at the hotel, Synthia had allowed the television to watch her drop off to sleep. Glancing at the clock, Synthia realized that she would have ample time for a long shower and perhaps, even a little bite to eat. She looked toward the night table, attempting to locate the room-service menu. Reaching over the bed, she lifted the menu from its stand and had a healthy yawn. After a quick perusal, Synthia set the menu on the bed and leaned forward to retrieve her robe from the foot of the bed. She did a couple of toe lifts to get the circulation going and then made her way to the bathroom. A small growl from her stomach caused Synthia to take one more backward glance at the tempting menu.

Perhaps I'll just grab a quick piece of fruit from the lobby café. Synthia had just finished brushing her teeth and was turning on the shower when she heard a knock at the door. Securing her robe, she walked to the door and inquired of her unexpected visitor.

"Room service, ma'am."

Synthia opened the door, leaving the security bar intact. "Do you have the right room? I didn't place any order."

"Yes, ma'am, this is the correct room. The hotel was given specific instructions to make sure that your stay was as pleasant as possible and that we were to anticipate all your needs."

Indeed, Synthia's flight and hotel was fully funded by Joseph Franklin. She opened the door allowing the overflowing breakfast table to roll into the room.

"Just how many people was this prepared for?" asked Synthia, her eyes wide.

"We weren't sure, ma'am. We were just told to include our full menu, even if you only wanted a bowl of cereal."

Synthia laughed. "All right, just leave it there I guess. Wait here while I get my purse."

The waiter immediately raised his hands. "No, ma'am," he said. "We were also given very strict orders that no money was to leave your hands. Everything has been taken care of. Enjoy your breakfast as well as your stay."

Synthia walked out of the golden doors of the small but luxurious hotel and observed a beautiful, graying morning sky. A doorman politely stepped forward.

"Ms Pearson?"

"Why, yes I'm she," said Synthia. The doorman waved his hand and immediately a midnight-blue Escalade made its way to the entranceway circle. A casually dressed driver got out and made his way toward Synthia.

"Ms. Pearson, I presume?"

"I'm *Mrs.* Pearson."

"Please allow me to take your bag, ma'am." Synthia did not refuse his courtesy. She handed her small travel bag to the driver.

"My name is Fletcher," he said. "I'll be your driver as well as your assistant for the day. Whatever you need, you only have to ask."

"Why thank you, Fletcher. My, I had almost forgotten about good manners."

"It's always easy when in the presence of a true lady."

"Um." Synthia was impressed. "Are you related to Mr. Franklin?" Fletcher gave her look of puzzlement. "Never mind," said Synthia, smiling.

Fletcher extended his hand toward Synthia and said, "Shall we go?" He held both the door and Synthia's hand as she stepped into the plush rear seat of her conveyance.

"Are all your shuttles like this?" she asked.

"Actually, yes." He made sure that she was safely inside before he shut the door. "It won't be too long a drive, Mrs. Pearson, but please feel free to browse the selection of music. You can either choose a song or just select a radio station. You'll find the menu screen directly in front of you."

"I'm sure that you know the best local stations, Fletcher. I'll let you select it for me."

"My pleasure, ma'am."

Synthia was enjoying the view as well as the friendly chatter and pleasing music of a local radio broadcast. When traveling, she always enjoyed the opportunity to briefly connect to the culture and flavor of that region. About twenty-five minutes into the ride, the vehicle arrived at a private roadway. Fletcher typed on a small keyboard that was located on the dashboard. Immediately the security gate that blocked the road slid open. The Escalade made its way along the road, going through several more turns upon the graveled track. After a sharp left turn, the road took a noticeable downward incline. Synthia soon recognized a new scent in the air: they were near water.

They came upon a simple docking area that harbored an impressive ferry. Although relatively small by commercial ferry standards, it made up for it with a unique and luxurious style. Two luxury vehicles were being driven into the lower cargo area of the vessel.

"Oh my!" said Synthia. "Do y'all ever buy anything from Wal-Mart?"

"I'm sorry, did you say something, ma'am?"

"Oh no… just thinking out loud."

"No problem, we're here." Once again, Fletcher did not allow Synthia to trouble herself with the door. He walked quickly around the car to offer his hand as if he were ensuring Cinderella's safe exit from her carriage. He took her bag and continued to escort his charge down to the ferry. Not one for casual contact with a stranger, Synthia nevertheless allowed the driver to hold her close when it appeared that the incline might affect her balance. They stepped up on the carpeted gangplank to board the ferry. Fletcher opened the door and Synthia immediately marveled at the expense of the décor and seating that met her eyes. There were no padded planks or iron benches here but four rows of tan-hued, leather captain chairs that were able to rotate 360 degrees and recline. Six tables were interspersed among the chairs. on closer inspection, Synthia realized that they were not simple tables: each one could be raised or lowered as well as extended. This allowed the option of private enjoyment with some cocoa or being able to have a lively game of cards with others. Each table also boasted various outlets and ports to satisfy even the most active of technophiles. Synthia leaned back into the chair. She almost cursed out loud when her hand accidentally pushed away the top of her right armrest. It slid forward to reveal the various options for a full chair massage.

"Welcome aboard, Mrs. Godbold-Pearson. My name is Captain Meeks." Synthia turned to respond to the formal salutation. Her eyes fell upon the salt-lined face of the ferry's captain. The hair on his head was full and cotton-white. It was joined on his face with the almost mandatory beard of a seasoned seafarer.

"Thank you very much, Captain Meeks. You have a wonderful vessel. I have never been on a five-star ferry before."

Captain Meeks laughed. "Well, I will make every effort not to disappoint you. I have two other men who take care of the ship's functions, but Fletcher here is very familiar with everything. I have full confidence that he can handle any of your needs. Just as a matter of information, the head…I'm sorry, the ladies' room can be found directly to your left, near the peach-colored sconce." He pointed. "I know that you are aware of some of the, let's say, precautions regarding the academy. With that in mind, I will tell you that pretty soon the blinds will draw shut and, unfortunately, you'll lose a wonderful view. Rest assured, the lighting will automatically adjust. We have wonderful distractions throughout the room." He gestured toward the amenities. "The refrigerator and juice bar is fully stocked, and since I know that Fletcher wouldn't mention it, I will tell you that he is an expert gourmet chef in case you desire a tempting snack. We should be reaching Cushsons Island in good order. I'll be down pretty soon to check on you. I was personally informed by Mr. Franklin that you are a special guest and that nothing less than a queen's care should be extended."

Synthia blushed as she waddled in Captain Meek's last comment. "I'm certainly no queen, Captain. You needn't worry about me, I'll be fine. I'll just probably catch up on CNN and, perhaps, read the newspaper." She shuddered at the thought of her newspaper.

"What's wrong?" Captain Meeks looked concerned. "I just remembered that I left my newspaper in the hotel lobby." Captain Meeks smiled as Fletcher got up from his chair and walked to the game board cupboard and procured four newspapers.

"What would you like to start with?" he said. "The *New York Times* or the *Philadelphia Inquirer?*"

CHAPTER TWENTY-SIX

Cushsons Island was one of the many islands formed in what is now the state of Maryland. It was privately purchased in 1949 by an African-American businessman, Cameron Soquelle. For many years Soquelle had struggled hard as a shipping businessman. He had overcome the perpetual perception of inferior reliability and quality that anchored many men of color. It did not ultimately hinder his monumental success during his forty-three years of business.

Soquelle had a strong desire to find a place where he could, at least temporarily, proclaim his world as free from hate. Through the ensuing years, Soquelle formed personal and formal relationships with other African-Americans of means. Collectively, they forged a small enclave of homes and supportive structures that allowed them a well-deserved respite from American life. By the mid-1960s, the beautiful Cushsons Island had developed into a sophisticated ensemble of fine estates. The true phenomenon of the island was that it remained an enigma to most outsiders. Unlike many other established islands of the wealthy, where human activity was highly visible, there were no events to be witnessed by jet-setters. For the most part, Cushsons Island was perceived to be essentially uninhabited. At times rumors surfaced identifying the island as a governmental property for juvenile detention. Remarks comparing to the island to an Alcatraz-like institution were mentioned. Perceptions were so skewed that it did not matter if, occasionally, people observed young black people on a passing boat seeming to have a grand time. The assigned rationale was influenced by the mind's belief that the children were happy because they were temporarily away from their detention areas. Who wouldn't be happy?

The underground corridors of New Passage Academy stood silent in their nocturnal watch over the sleeping school. The only sound heard was the moans from a well-matured, functional furnace that permeated the hallway, disturbing the reverie of the solemn night.

The academy was a structural work of genius. On the surface, its educational buildings mimicked the façade of a high-end residential development. There were no walls, pillars, or smokestacks to give one visual pause. It stood as a gated, residential haven of the well-endowed.

The development consisted of thirty elegant homes. Twelve of the homes served non-traditional functions. To enter one home was to enter an expansive library and media center. It even boasted a lecture room for guests of the international academia. Another home served as a scientific laboratory center, a sister to an adjoining biology home. Students were able to access the various buildings by way of the underground access corridors. These corridors were themselves high-tech structures complete with shiny walls, recessed lights, and multiple communication pots. Various works of art also lined the walkway. The lighting was especially bright, intentionally done to minimize the negative emotional effects of being underground.

A proud feat of the school was that the last upgrade of the underground corridor had been entirely designed by the students—the ninth-grade students. The upperclassmen were too busy working on redesigning a robotic prosthesis. Fifteen-year-old Rowenia had embedded visual implants in the legs that would act as a Seeing Eye dog and passively steer its owner away from danger. She had even temporarily, and illegally, hacked her way into the government satellite systems so she could utilize its more sophisticated not-for consumer-use GPS system. Now the legs would not only avoid obstacles, they could also find their way around or toward any destination.

Mindful of the need for fresh air and sunlight, a community pool and recreational center was also part of the property. All of the non-academic residents of the community were aware of the academy's presence, all supportive of its purpose.

Alone in his private home Brodrey Toomers sat perched on his white shower stool. He let the cool water continue its unrelenting rain upon his head and back. For many years Brodrey had convinced himself that he had purged his lustful appetite for young males. Even when a hint of perversion sought to rise from within the now balding man, he immersed himself in an activity or project that served to busy his mind. Lately, Toomers realized that he was losing the battle. At times he found himself watching students as they passed by in the corridors. Sometime ago he found his heart leaping when he looked up. He believed that he had seen the school's custodian peering at him in a strange fashion. Toomers didn't know whether he had been caught or not. He quickly sought a private area in the academy's atrium to quell his racing thoughts.

Today, he awakened with firmness in his loins. Even in deep sleep, his thoughts served to activate his body's glands, which caused a rigid response. As the evening came, Toomers realized that he was approaching a total relapse. The chilled water was doing nothing to restrain the malevolent tugging that now dismissed all reason. His coiled thoughts focused on LeDain Sanford.

A month earlier, Toomers had come across the young man in the library's expansive media. LeDain was accessing information for a research project. He hadn't noticed the presence of Professor Toomers until he heard breathing behind him.

"Hello, Professor Toomers. I didn't see you come in. You scared me." LeDain looked around the media center to see if they were alone. Twice now he had spotted the professor peering at classmates in an odd way. It was nothing serious or provocative, but LeDain's heart told him that all was not well. He had covertly inquired of his classmates if they thought that Professor Toomers was odd. The only answers he received pertained to the professor's propensity for pop quizzes and agonizingly long presentations. No one offered any clues regarding untoward remarks or advances, nor did LeDain ask directly. For a moment Professor Toomers just stood there almost as if he were admiring the work of his young student. LeDain looked around and noticed one other student present: Gabrielle. Gabrielle was wearing a headset and appeared to be engrossed in a multiplayer Scrabble Board Tournament. She was determined to uphold her crown. Gabrielle's opponents would probably be devastated if she had posted her real picture and not one from a stock file. It would not sit well with the adult level players to know that she was actually an eleven-year-old girl.

LeDain stole another glance in Gabrielle's direction and then turned to face Professor Toomers.

"Good afternoon to you, young man," said Professor Toomers. "Getting all the information you need?"

"Yes. Yes, sir," said LeDain. "I'm almost finished here, and then I have to go to meet up with my study group."

"Oh, I didn't know that they had study group on Saturdays. We can't work you students all the time."

"No, this is one that we made up ourselves. We're studying primitive regional languages. We're trying to see if one was more predisposed to tribal dissension versus the other. You know, did we change with our speech, or did our speech eventually change us?"

"Very interesting. I'm looking forward to the group's conclusions," said Professor Toomers as he gently touched LeDain's left shoulder. He allowed his right hand to move across the back of the boy's neck before he gave a gentle squeeze. Toomers' mind thrust into ways to maneuver the student from the room. His right hand had returned to LeDain's shoulder while his left hand had found its way into his pocket. He knew that it would be difficult to get the boy to respond to his wishes but his sexual depravity served to partially convince him that perhaps there was a way. The professor's eyes were still on the computer monitor. His thoughts increased his sense of arousal. *The hell with it. I can get him out of here.* He took his hand out of his pocket and grabbed hold of LeDain.

"Whoopee!" Gabrielle was excited. She looked around the room to see who was available to join her in her new victory. Professor Toomers snapped his hands quickly to either side. He stepped backward so as not to give the appearance of being too close to the boy. Professor Toomers pointed at the monitor as if his purpose for standing there was to assist the ambitious student. After directing a silent curse in the direction of Gabrielle, he departed from the media center without another word.

Toomer's thought returned to the present. He reached up to turn off the water flow and walked out of the shower and over to his computer. He didn't bother to towel dry.

CHAPTER **TWENTY-SEVEN**

Synthia walked along the corridors of New Passage Academy with her assigned escort, Sebastian Tisdale. Sebastian was pleased to have company on the school grounds and was making every effort to impress his charming guest. Suddenly Sebastian stopped in his tracks. He had an odd look on his face and appeared to be attempting to slow his breathing. He gathered himself in an attempt to return to his conversation regarding the school. Once again Sebastian stopped mid-sentence, clutching his stomach. Synthia noticed a thin film of sweat glistening on his forehead.

Earlier that day Sebastian had begun antibiotics to combat an ear infection. Combined with a suspect pudding at lunch, the concoction had begun an internal symphony.

"Please wait here." He excused himself and moved posthaste in the direction of the closest porcelain sanctuary. Synthia admired the paintings on the wall as she patiently waited for Sebastian to return. She heard the sounds of multiple footsteps coming her way. A small group of young girls and boys were being led by a pleasant-looking older gentleman. The group appeared jovial as the teacher walked and discussed the important history of some of the art pieces that graced the walls.

"Why hello," said the teacher to Synthia. "Are you being helped?"

"Hello to you, thanks for asking, but I'm fine. Sebastian had to make a pit stop, so I'm waiting for him to return." The students were staring at Synthia, obviously surprised to see a stranger in this exclusive domain.

"Is she someone's mom?" said a soft voice.

"I like those earrings," said a well-dressed girl.

Synthia made small talk with the teacher and his class. She noticed that one of the boys stood off by himself, leaning against a plant table. He was looking up at the artwork, jotting down some notes. The handsome young man finished his notes and was nonchalantly making his way back to the crowd. For a moment, Synthia lost track of him as she conversed with the other students. Suddenly, she noticed that the young man was next to her yet he was looking elsewhere. He finally turned to Synthia.

"Pleased to meet you, ma'am," he said, extending his hand. Synthia smiled and reached out her hand to greet the shy boy. It was then that she noticed that something was touching her hand. She realized that the boy was putting a piece of paper in her hand. Although tempted to address the boy, the journalist in her instinctively kept up the subterfuge and fully covered the folded paper with her hand. She continued her conversation with a couple of the curious girls as if nothing had happened.

"Oh, what wonderful manners you all have." Synthia could not explain it, but she knew not to look at the paper or make a comment. She merely kept smiling and nodding at the entire group, although she did attempt to steal a glance at her young co-conspirator. He seemed to be about nine years old. Like the others, he was sharply dressed and well-groomed.

"Well," said the group's teacher, "I see Mr. Tisdale coming our way, so why don't we give our guest a break and move along, shall we?" Synthia said her goodbyes to the departing group. As they rounded the corner to access the elevators, her young friend slowed down, daring one last look at the news anchorwoman.

"Come now, Mr. Sanford," said the teacher. The child ventured one last smile and walked away.

"Sorry to keep you waiting," said Sebastian. "Just not myself today. I see that you met some of our fine students."

"Yes, they are a wonderful group of young men and women. Tell me, are all the students content here at the academy? More importantly, how difficult is it for a child to leave if he so desires?" Synthia was not aware of the content of the mysterious note, but somehow the line of questioning seemed to be appropriate. An oblivious Sebastian quickly answered her question.

"We find that students here are very content. Every now and then a student, for whatever reason, does not fit in. It is rare, but still, it does happen. We then simply escort them back home."

"What, with their heads covered in the middle of night for secrecy?"

"Oh no, nothing as dramatic as that. We do make sure that travel is at night. We keep things, shall we say, low-key. As I'm sure that you've noticed, this community is not easily accessible. I also remind you that water has a way of swaying one's orientation."

Synthia's curiosity regarding the note was becoming increasingly elevated. Still, she dared not remove it until she was certain of her privacy.

"So how long have you been here, Sebastian?"

"About eleven years I guess."

"And how do you like it?"

"I like it just fine. It's a fabulous place. It has also allowed me to travel, not to mention purchase my dream car."

"Hmm, maybe I'd better put an application in here," said Synthia. "What problems do you have at this place?"

"Problems, what do you mean?"

"Come on, every place has problems. You're saying that this place is paradise?"

"No, it's certainly not paradise. Anywhere there are people there are problems, but we usually straighten things out very quickly."

Synthia eased closer to her guide. "Things, what kind of things?"

"My, you are a reporter, aren't you? At times we get problems among the teaching professionals. It's nothing too big or that can't be worked out." He looked around before he continued. "What I will say is that in the past five years or so the, shall we say...the place has changed. Oh, nothing that one can really put one's finger on. It's just that sometimes, during our meetings and such, there is a mild but growing separation of philosophy among the staff. Even some of the administrators appear to be forming predictable cliques. Some of the faculty believes that it's time to formally summon some of our silent yet distant leadership."

"And where do you stand, Sebastian?" Sebastian realized that he had probably already said too much. He folded his hands as he leaned against the wall. The line of questioning triggered his gastric juices to slowly agitate the pot. Taking a long look at his guest, he momentarily debated his conversational course. Something about this woman granted permission for him to share feelings that had troubled him more than he realized. Taking a deep breath, he said: "I can't put my finger on the true problem, Mrs. Pearson. What I have come to sense is that the conversation regarding our students has changed. It's just that I don't hear the same type of encouraging academic comments or quarterly plans that used to be the order of the day. Don't get me wrong, the good work is still going on; it's just that the enthusiasm of faculty partnering has changed." Sebastian absentmindedly rubbed his patient stomach. "Perhaps we do need a 'Come to Jesus' meeting from the real leaders of this ship. We'll see." He looked at Synthia. "Maybe they're at work already."

"Why, has there been increased travel to the island?" Synthia studied him.

"No, not really. Actually, I haven't seen anyone come in for a while now. Come to think of it..." He paused to confirm his thoughts.

"What, what is it?" said Synthia. "Come to think of what?"

Sebastian gave her an odd look. "Well, it's not really a problem, but I can't remember any recent trips or departures by any of the students. Yes, it's been a while since anyone has left here."

"You don't see that as a problem?"

"No, not as a problem. As a matter of fact, it could simply mean that indeed all is well."

Synthia said nothing as she held her stare toward Sebastian. "Perhaps it is something that you may want to look into, Mr. Tisdale."

"Perhaps it is. Maybe I will do just that. Yes, I will do just that." He smiled again.

"It's getting late, Mrs. Pearson, and I apologize for not being in top form, but it's probably best that I call it a day."

"That's quite all right, Sebastian. You have been more than gracious. I am very pleased to have met you."

"The pleasure has been all mine." He blushed. "I trust that this will not be your last visit to our esteemed institution."

"Only if you promise to be my guide again." Sebastian's stomach was already feeling better.

"Got a moment?" Fellyard Beedly leaned against the door frame. Toomers' heart jumped as he turned to the doorway. *Wasn't that locked?* he thought. He hesitantly welcomed Fellyard in with a wave of his hand.

"Why of course, Mr. Beedley. I always have a moment for you."

"Thank you, Brodrey-boy, you are always so obliging. I know that you're busy, that you have other things on your mind, so I shan't keep you."

"Oh no, time's not a problem, is everything all right?" Toomers' hand began to shake as he lifted his water glass. He quickly set it back down.

"It's funny that you should ask that, Brodrey. It was my exact question to you." Fellyard was now walking in a somewhat circular pattern towards Toomers' desk. This did not help Toomers in his attempt to quell his tremors. He glanced at his telephone, gauging the probability of a successful call for assistance. The thought was immediately and wisely dismissed.

"Brodrey, my good fellow, are you well? I hope I didn't catch you on a bad day." He moved directly in front of Toomers, leaning down until their eyes were just four inches away from each other. Toomers had to will his blood to keep flowing, to warm a body that seemed to grow strangely cold. Fellyard's piercing gaze held Toomers. He spoke through clenched teeth.

"We must talk."

CHAPTER TWENTY-EIGHT

Soft vocals flowed from the Quam speakers in Synthia's home office. She attempted to relax as Michael Henderson implored her to *Be My Girl*. She paused in her movements as she quietly appreciated his manly baritone. Peabo Bryson soon took his turn on the microphone. He pushed Synthia to *Feel the Fire*. His vocals gave Synthia temporary respite from the problems of the day. Her hands were folded on her lap as the pleasing a cappella sound of The Persuasions entered the room. She gently nodded along with the unique harmonies of the singers. It wasn't until the second verse that her mind picked up on the actual lyrics of the song. It was The Persuasions' rendition of *Half of my Blood is Cain's Blood, Half of my Blood is Abel's*.

Synthia's thoughts kept returning to Chadric. She could wait no longer. She didn't want to pick a fight nor did she want to raise false accusations, but this was too important a matter to leave unaddressed. Too many things had happened over the past few days: she could not stand any more riddles. Disturbing thoughts had already caused several nights of unsettling sleep. Synthia had finally found the love of her life: could he already be a stranger? Slowly, she eased back her desk chair and stood up to leave her office. Even as she walked toward the kitchen area, her mind offered options to re-think her steps. *Perhaps he'll tell me soon or, c'mon Synthia, it's probably nothing.* Synthia kept walking.

She found Chadric in the small storage area next to the kitchen. He was kneeling on the floor next to his toolbox. She could see that he was adjusting his utility knife. A pack of shiny razor-sharp blades lay opened on the floor.

"Honey, there's something that I've been meaning to ask you. At first I thought that it was no big deal, but now I just have to know." Chadric finished testing the lever of the utility knife, confirming its proper setting. He had the knife in his hands as he slowly turned toward her.

"Sure, love. What do you want to know, is there some problem?"

She hesitated, wondering what required repairing in their well-kept home.

"It's about our honeymoon." He raised an eyebrow but said not a word. *What could have been wrong with the honeymoon?* he thought.

"Sweetie, during our honeymoon, I saw you talking to a man in the lobby of our hotel. At first I thought nothing of it. I simply believed that you had met a fellow tourist and you were making friendly small talk." He stopped toying with the knife's lever, but he did not put it down. He continued to listen to his wife.

"Sometime later it hit me that I had seen that man before. He was at our wedding. There's something not quite right about that man. I have to know, who is he to you and how did he happen to be in Hawaii?" He gave her no answer, only manipulated of the knife's blade. She could tell that he was struggling to make some sort of response. *But why does there need to be a struggle?* she thought. She jumped as she saw the knife move through the air. It took only a millisecond for her to mentally process the fact that he had merely tossed the utility knife into his toolbox.

"Think I'll leave that ship repair for later." Synthia had almost forgotten about her husband's hobby of making model ships. He often required a sharp blade to make the final trimmings. He drew in a long breath and set the toolbox down on top of a small countertop.

"What's wrong, honey? Please talk to me."

"Let's go in the kitchen to talk about this. I'm wanting a little coffee for this one." Synthia followed Chadric into the kitchen where he washed his hands and began to prepare a fresh pot of coffee.

She could see that he was still in deep thought. She began to feel very afraid of what she was about to hear. He did not wait for the coffee to brew. He slid one of the kitchen chairs over and sat next to her, meeting her eyes.

"Baby, there are a few things that I need to share with you. It is not that I was trying to keep anything from you; it's just that there are some things in my life that I have long since buried." For almost a minute the kitchen remained silent save for the rhythmic burping of the brewing coffee pot. He found his voice and began to speak.

"First of all, I don't know why Fellyard Beedley was at our wedding. That's his name: Fellyard Beedley. I certainly did not invite him, and if anyone asked, he probably told them that I was his nephew. I am not. Beedley called all the children his nephew or his niece."

"All the children? All of what children, Chadric? What are you talking about?"

"Synthia, I know that you have been on a mission these past few weeks regarding a secret educational academy."

"Yes dear, you know everyone's buzzing about it. I even got a chance to visit the place. It's very impressive, but other things are starting to happen. That's why I've made contact with the authorities. I'll be meeting with a detective soon. I just couldn't say anything before, you understand?"

He touched her hand and said, "Yes, I understand your job. I know that some things cannot be shared right away, even with me. We discussed it before. I also understand and know that New Passage Academy has done and can do amazing and wonderful things." She sat upright and stared at her husband. How was he so knowledgeable about the academy?

"What do you mean, *you know?* Don't tell me that you've visited the place before—when?"

Chadric got up to pour his coffee. He returned to the table and took a cautious sip before replying. "Synthia, I didn't visit New Passage Academy. I'm a graduate." For a long time she did not even blink. She stared at her husband. She was stunned and without words to respond.

Chadric continued. "Yes love, your husband was one of those children who were signed over to a non-existent academy." Synthia finally found a voice, but could not decide on the words.

She felt her lips drying as anger began to take first place in her new swarm of emotions. The lie of omission did its work, quickly convincing Synthia that only more lies and deceit were in store for her.

"I can't believe that you would keep something like this from me—why! What else is there in your life that's a secret from Synthia? Were you married before, any little Chadrics that I should know about?"

Synthia's voice wavered with the last comment. It was a remark designed to hurt but still possessed the potential to return to the giver a heart-hollowing answer.

"Just wait a minute!" yelled Chadric

"No, you wait a minute! I've been hurt enough and I don't need this in my life!"

"Need what in your life? Perhaps you've been on TV too long. Not everything has to be drama."

"Don't you dare patronize me! I'm not gonna sit here and take your…"

A flush-faced Chadric jerked from his chair, unaware that he had just missed dumping the hot coffee over everything.

"Can you just wait and listen? Don't talk, just listen!"

"Oh now you're telling me what to do? The hell with you, I'm not the one with the dark secrets!" Synthia's eyes narrowed as a small amount of fluid threatened to escape from her nostril.

"I thought that we had something Chadric, that we shared everything. If we can't trust each other with the truth, then what's the point; how do we go on?"

"Whoa there Synthia," said Chadric as he slowly returned to a sitting position. "I'm sorry, I truly am." He reached across the table toward the hands of his trembling wife. "But every secret does not have to be sinister. It wasn't, isn't about deceiving you, but keeping me—we still go on."

Synthia had not allowed Chadric to clasp her hand as he tried again to make physical contact. She pulled her hands back and crossed her arms across her breast. Her slow-rocking motion and flared nostrils gave Chadric a clear signal that the domestic battle remained at a critical level. Chadric did not remove his extended hand but softly turned it so his palm was in an upward position. "Not every secret is dark, some are just painful. I wish that life could be a storybook Synthia, but very few lives are. To be completely honest, keeping it in was the only way that I could come to grips with things. Was just trying to keep my own sanity." He didn't allow himself to look at Synthia's still glaring eyes— had they softened some? "Oh, I know the mantra is to release everything that is inside, to not surpass one's hurts and all that bullshit.

"Best believe that everyone who says it is still holding on to something real tight and real close. Just want you to read their lips. I ain't no better, no worse than most." Synthia's professional personality forced her to hold onto her anger; she would not quickly surrender it, regardless of anyone's comments. Betrayal-laced emotions dared not allow her to rein in her sharpened fury. Another voice managed to whisper, reminding her of some of her own missteps of the past; misguided treks along long smothered paths of devilish adventure. No, she hadn't shared all of those simple-minded days and just plain foolish nights with her husband.

But that was different, wasn't it?

Chadric returned his focus toward the coffee cup, allowing the tension in the air to join the rising vapors in its slow dissipation. He was still looking down when he heard his wife's voice.

"You could have told me Chadric." Chadric heart surrendered some of its heaviness but he still did not raise his eyes from the coffee cup. He silently admitted that he was afraid to look at his wife and possibly give permission for his own emotions to run unchecked. It wasn't that he was afraid to bear his feelings to his wife, but was terrified of ripping the scar that had held fast his damaged soul. He spoke both to his wife and to his untouched coffee.

"Honey, my hesitation to share wasn't really about New Passage Academy, but what happened to me there."

"I don't, still don't know what to believe Chadric. I don't know what to say. Why did you keep this from me?"

"Believe me, boo, it wasn't because I wanted to deceive you. That wasn't it at all."

"But, but you told me that you graduated from Rothsford Preparatory School before you went on to Cornell. Was that all a lie?" Synthia had ceased her rocking motion but her guard remained in the high defense position. She loved this man who sat in front of her. She just needed to know who he was. He took her hand.

"Synthia, I am your husband, your lover. I am not a liar. Yes, that is a chapter of my life that I kept from you. I didn't share it with you because of the nature of the school and because of what almost happened to me there."

"What, what happened?" She was not certain that her swirling head could take anymore, but she had to know it all. The telephone rang, its tone hollow and threatening in the silent room. Neither moved to answer it. They realized that this was one of those times when all attention was required for the issue at hand; the world would have to wait.

"I attended, but I didn't actually graduate from the Academy," Chadric continued. "I wasn't trying to add a lie. It's just that I did spend most of my school years at New Passage. I kinda feel like a graduate." He fingered the rim of his mug. "I am indeed a graduate of Rothsford Preparatory School. I transferred from New Passage Academy in the spring of my junior year." He sipped his coffee, realizing that it had become lukewarm, losing its invigorating powers. He sat the mug down and stared at Synthia's hands. She could tell that he was still searching for words. The search was not without pain.

"There was a problem with one of the teachers at the academy," he said. "It was a teacher who tried to convince me to share some time with him, in his bed with him." Chadric grew silent. He chose to study the hypnotic movement of his watch's second-hand. After two revolutions, he continued his story.

"It never got that far. You know, in the bed. While we were walking together toward his home, I ran away from him. I hid in my room the entire night. The next day I made my way to my section dean's office to report everything. When I walked into the office, the dean was not there. At his desk was a man who stopped by the academy on occasion to lecture on world geography. His name was Fellyard Beedley, the man you saw at our wedding." He looked into her wide eyes. "For the life of me I don't know how, but he found me in Hawaii. I think he told me something about a world conference on global warming or something. His expertise is geography, so who knows? I'm still trying to figure out how, after all of these years, he can still get around so well. I thought he was ancient when I was in high school." He swallowed the lump in his throat. "But anyway, he's sitting at the dean's desk. I explain to him all that had happened with the professor. I told him that something was wrong with the professor and that he was up to no good. Beedley comforted me and assured me that he was going to handle everything. He said there would be no more trouble from the professor. Of course I felt all better and was hoping to hear that the professor was gone. I never thought to check with anyone else. Fellyard Beedley was not at the school often, but he had a take-charge way about him." He wasn't sure how Synthia was receiving this. "The next day I get a message that I'm being transferred to another academy. They said that all would be fine and my father would not have to pay any money. I guess Beedley thinks that I owe him for saving me from molestation. Fact of the matter is that I loved the academy and believed that the professor was the one who would be leaving. I did nothing wrong. I tried to talk to someone else but Beedley had already set things up. What did I know? From time to time I would see Joseph Franklin at the academy. He's the one that I really wanted to speak with, but he hadn't been around for more than five months. Come to think of it, Beedley was never there if Mr. Franklin was at the academy. I missed Mr. Franklin. He was always an easy adult to speak with."

"But, Chadric, how did you ever get to be at the academy? I thought that you said that after your parents died, you lived with a rich uncle." He bit down on his teeth, his jaws clenched and quivering. "What else could I say, Synthia? I had to fill in the holes someway. Truth of the matter is that I don't know whether my father is dead or alive. I wish that I knew. I'd like to tell him that all is well." He lifted his bowed head to address his wife. "Synthia, I was sent to the school by my father. Not because he didn't love me, but because he felt he had no other choice. It was my mother who had fallen victim to the streets. My father was a hard-working man who didn't have much. Like many others, he just could never get ahead. There was always something that would reach out and snatch whatever small savings he could muster. I didn't understand it all then, but I do recall hearing him and my mother fight." He had figured that he would have to share his past with Synthia one day, but he never imagined it would be this soon.

"Many of the things from our house went missing. My mother would come home late at night, sometimes not at all. Dad would then come in from his second job and find out that I had been alone all through the night. Worn to the bone, dad would pick me up and give me a bath and then prepare me something hot to eat. Even though he would be smiling at me, he would also be muttering and cursing under his breath. I knew that he was thinking about my mother." He paused to remember his father standing over the stove. "Sometimes dad would come home at night and find my mother in a drunken stupor, lying across the bed. He would summon his spent energy and come to my school because he knew that I had left home with no lunch money, even though he used to leave me money on the dresser by my bed. But he soon realized that I would never see it come morning. Things soon got so bad with my mother that she would soon do anything for drug money."

He looked at Synthia then down at his hands. "It finally happened. One night dad was too worn out to even go to his night job so he came straight home." Chadric leaned back in his chair and closed his eyes. "Dad had stopped by the deli to pick up a hoagie so we could eat and talk some. When he got home he found me half asleep on the downstairs sofa. Before he could wave the hoagie under my nose, he heard mom and her friend upstairs. Dad raced upstairs to find two men in bed with his wife. One was doing his business while the other guy was putting a tourniquet on her arm. She didn't care. Without saying a word, Dad left the door open and came downstairs and gathered me up. He placed me in the rear seat of his rusty van and told me to wait."

Chadric remembered the day all too well. He chose his words with caution. "Dad went back into the house, walked to the circuit breaker and turned off all the power. He then yelled toward the upstairs bedroom to say that he was going to be back in thirty minutes and if anyone was still in the house, they would be enjoying darkness from that day forward. My mother was still high from the heroin, but the men quickly understood the raw resolve of a wronged husband. They hurried their steps. Even as Dad's van was halfway down the street, the men were rushing their way out of the house with my mother stumbling behind them. It wasn't that she believed that dad would cause her harm, she just wanted to stay close to her suppliers.

"My father and I spent the night at a friend's home. My poor father had taken the night off work because he was physically spent, yet he still had to stay up half the night. We returned to our house in the morning. My father placed my mother's belonging by the front door. She never got them." He didn't think it would be this easy to talk to Synthia about his past. "A few days later my mother was arrested for the attempted robbery of a gas station. She and her two friends were so out of it that they tried to rob the station while on foot, not even with a getaway car. The attendant had refused to turn his money over to the three obviously compromised addicts, whose only weapons were ice picks." He stared but didn't see anything. "The station attendant had grabbed a bat and began to chase my mother and her brainiac friends down the street. The attendant easily caught up with my mother. He threw her to the ground. One of her friends—worried not for her safety but her ability to barter for drugs—returned to help. After a struggle, the attendant wound up with an ice pick in his back. He survived, but my mother and her buddies had to do some time. My mother got two years. While still in prison, and just before parole, she managed to pick a fight with the wrong person. She never made it out...at least, not walking." Synthia looked at her husband to gauge his response to the memory of his mother's demise. She could not sense an emotion one way or the other. The dearth of emotion actually served to give Synthia more pain. She patiently listened as her husband continued his story.

"I don't know where her body is," said Chadric. "I have no idea. But even before she went to prison, my father and I struggled together. He just didn't know what to do. It seemed like trouble would always be his sleeping blanket. Oh, he tried to hide the problems from me, but I knew he still needed to have two jobs just so's we could live with some sort of decency." Synthia quietly observed the phenomenon of recalled pain. Her husband was highly educated and possessed a gift of conversational eloquence, yet his speech pattern had reverted to a form that was used in a household long ago. Chadric absentmindedly sipped the cold coffee and continued. "I knew that dad was at his wits' end for not knowing how to care for me. I saw him getting older and older every day. Seemed like every time he came back through the door, he had left another piece of his spirit outside.

"Then one night it all changed. That was the night there was a loud knock on the door. Dad cussed because he assumed it was someone looking for payment of an outstanding bill. Bill collectors couldn't call anymore because the phone had been cut off. But at the door was a well-dressed man who respectfully introduced himself to dad as he eased his way into the house. At first I could tell that my father was suspicious, but the man had a way of talking that finally got to my dad, settling his mind. I heard a lot of back and forth. At one point it sounded like my dad was getting mad at the man. When I got the nerve to peek around the corner, I thought that I saw my father crying. He then put his head down in his hands. It seemed like he was trying to hold the whole world and all its problems in his shaking hands, so it wouldn't bust out." He closed his eyes. "My father then looks at the man and whispered yes. I still didn't know what was going on. But later on that evening my father called me to his side to sit for a spell. We talked for a long time and then we both cried. I, I saw my father twice after that, Synthia. I don't know what really happened, still can't explain it. He told me that he loved me, but so much of who he was as a man had been lost in the past ten years. We sat in a diner, Synthia, he was ashamed of his own home—our home. As we sat there with cold fries and untouched cheeseburgers, he told me that he was going to move to Virginia. He wanted to see if he could find work with his cousin at the plant there. He said that it was time to get his self right, to be a man, a real father. I told him that I had a real father and that I would leave the school and go with him." He sighed. "He almost turned that table over, Synthia. He told me that to do that would make him feel like he had failed in everything that he had touched, and the only thing that brought him smiles at night was the fact that I was in a good school and headed for a good life. He told me that he would be happy to chase a factory in Virginia, knowing that I wouldn't have to. We just held each other in that diner, Synthia. He said that he was proud of me and that he always would be. He showed me his hands and told me that there was nothing shameful in a man making a living with his hands. He also told me that there ain't no shame in a man with smooth hands who works with his brain." Chadric flashed back to that afternoon in the diner.

"A good day's work is just that, Chadric, regardless of your trade. However, even a dummy like me understands that the ones with the smoother hands tend to make more money. Why not you?" his father said to him across the table.

"I don't care about the money. I want to be with you."

"I want to be with you too, son. Your dad just made some mistakes that were hard to get away from." He then looked at Chadric and smiled. "But you were never one of them, Chadric. I'm doing the best that I can do for you right now. We just both suck it in and do what we have to for now, till things get better. I'm sorry that I can't be the father that you want right now, but you can be the best son and go back to school. Learns all you can and then some. Don't be afraid of success. While people be looking for success, it's also looking for them. Let it find you, son. It'll see you quicker if I get out of the way."

"I never saw him again, Synthia. I once got a chance to check down in Virginia but they said he had long gone. Even spoke to a one-time lady friend of his. It seemed like she was quite fond of him. Dad had worked there for a while. She told me that he never seemed happy, even when he laughed." Chadric turned toward Synthia. "She didn't even know that he had a son, never spoke of me. I was angry when the lady mentioned that. But it kinda makes sense now. What she was saying was that he had wrapped his pain and frustration up so tight that he would never dare to share it lest it turned back to cut its owner. She told me that whatever had happened, my father was a good man but he needed convincing of that. I never found him, don't know if he's still alive. I'd like to tell him that it's all right…that no forgiveness is necessary. I'd like him to know that the son who he once carried into that dark night has now struggled into a good life. Synthia, my dream would be for me to be at the dinner table with my queen on one side and my father on the other. He's my father—a good father. I'd like to say thank you, that I still love you." Synthia said not a word. The room was blurred. She could not stop the tears that met her quivering chin. She moved her chair closer to Chadric and held her husband.

CHAPTER **TWENTY-NINE**

The pulsating flow from the brass shower head continued its downpour upon the back of Professor Brodrey Toomers. His breathing was slow and steady, his chest barely moving. Many times he had used the solitude of the shower to gain control of swirling thoughts and urges. The whispers that now gained prominence in his throbbing head spoke as not his own, yet somehow, still familiar. It was as if he had heard the voice throughout many years and only today did it choose to identify itself. The voice encouraged Toomers to dismantle all barriers that hindered the release of his long-hindered satisfaction. It reminded the tormented man that to deny his lust was to deny his very existence, that true happiness could only be found in the full expression of his true self. Toomers had suppressed his true essence for far too long. The gifted professor was steadily losing more and more of himself. His eyes no longer gave evidence of a man of education and distinction. His narrowed pupils flicked rapidly in each direction, uncertain of its destination. His breathing began to increase as his eyes narrowed on his pock-marked brow. The cold water had failed to decrease both his spiritual and physical body temperatures. Beads of pungent sweat joined to form rivulets that continued down the small of his back. He toweled down; his excreting skin still refusing to totally dry.

After getting dressed, he sat down on the floor of his bedroom to put on his shoes. Somehow the whispers were clearer when he was closer to the floor. Suddenly, it came to Toomers' understanding that his tenure as a professor of Applied Physics at New Passage Academy was over. He understood that his instructions from Fellyard were to remain and be an instrument of Fellyard's deviant change, but other voices were now exerting carnal pressures on his mind. Even the threat of Fellyard's anger, and not being available for future administrative manipulations, could not alter his direction. Nefarious awakenings now manifested sovereignty in his darkened spirit. Fellyard Beedley underestimated the fragility of Toomers' nature. Fellyard hadn't realized that Toomers was no longer fit for his assigned task. Toomers put on a droopy yard hat that partially obscured his eyes. In his pocket was a bowie knife, his shiny acquaintance of many years. He checked his wallet to ensure that he had ample funds for an extended trip. He picked up the phone to dial the emergency number for the academy's ferry.

It was 12:10 in the morning. LeDain Sanford was roughly awakened by Professor Brodrey Toomers. He shook the disoriented boy to the floor and made it clear that he was to get dressed in rapid fashion: Toomers reminded LeDain that he knew the whereabouts of his mother and showed LeDain the bowie knife. It served to reinforce his intentions of what he'd do to his mother if he did not do exactly as commanded.

LeDain finally steadied himself, intent on obeying all of the professor's instructions. Toomers pulled LeDain close to him until they were face to face. LeDain could barely look at him.

"You will do exactly as I say—exactly," said Toomers. "Anytime that I think that you intend to do anything else, I will make sure that you get the chance to speak to your brother."

Tears welled up in the eyes of LeDain. He still thought often of his dead brother. Toomers sprayed spittle on LeDain's face as he spoke and increased the pressure of his grip.

"Don't you dare go sissy on me, you little prick! I ain't finished talking to you just yet. What you especially need to know is that if you don't behave like I say, even if you run away from me, I will find you." His voice slowed down. He intentionally enhanced each syllable as he finished his threat: "But understand this, I won't look for you right away because I'll be directly on my way to see Miss Nora Sanford. After having danced with mommy, I'll then make it my job to track you down. It won't matter where you are or who you think is protecting you, one day I'll tap you on your little shoulder. Now what we're going to do is to take a little private ride to the doctor and get on that ferry. You will not say a word, I'll handle everything. You just remember mommy and whether you want to see her all laid out in front of the church."

Brodrey Toomers and LeDain Sanford arrived at the dock just in time to see the crew of the ferry completing their launch preparations. The ferry and its crew were always on alert for emergency situations. Through the years there were times that someone had to immediately leave the island community, mostly for medical reasons. New Passage Academy's community nurse would usually be the one to initiate an emergency procedure. Sometimes an evening trip to return a child to his parents or guardian was required, but it was usually a scheduled event.

As the two boarded the ferry, the crew easily recognized the academy's professor but were curious regarding the child that he held close. Toomers explained to the captain that LeDain had grown increasingly despondent regarding the recent death of his older brother and that the staff of New Passage Academy had tried all they could to console the young man. He let them know that the child had reached the point where he was now physically acting out his despair, a threat to others as well as himself. Such a shame. The young boy had become so distressed in the past twenty-four hours that a scheduled trip was not possible.

When Toomers had spoken of the death of LeDain's brother, the rest of the story fell into place. The crew respectfully gave the two passengers distance, acknowledging the tragic situation. Toomers obligingly nodded to the understanding crew.

The ferry reached land in short order. LeDain sat quietly in his chair. He entertained the idea of somehow getting help from one of the crew members but each time he looked up, the desperate eyes of Toomers met his gaze. He kept thinking of his mother and how, with Jared gone, she was the only one left to call family. LeDain thought briefly about his father and how, if he were alive, he'd be kicking the crap out of Professor Toomers. He quickly acknowledged that if his father were alive, they might all still be a family. He drifted off to sleep.

He was crudely awakened by the professor. Toomers made sure that his grip on LeDain was firm but not so overt or obvious as to call attention from the crew. Toomers had the captain call ahead for a taxi. The captain had informed him that it would be easier to contact the limo service that was contracted by the academy. Toomers explained that that was not necessary and that he had already inconvenienced enough people for one night. The compassionate captain then offered his own car keys to Toomers.

"Here, take my vehicle, it's the black Dodge Ram truck parked near the dock. I'll get a ride with one of the crew if I need to. Actually, I'll probably just spend the rest of the night on board. Hell, the cabins are better than my own bedroom." Toomers grabbed the keys.

"Are you sure?"

"It's fine," said the captain. "If I still need a ride in the morning, I'll contact our transportation service." The captain had barely finished his sentence before Toomers had turned around and was hurrying out the door. *Poor young man, thought the captain, he looks so distraught and afraid. I wish that there was something that I could do.*

CHAPTER **THIRTY**

Reverend Sydney leaned back in his chair, drawing a few deep breaths before his afternoon appointment with Sister Quentella Snowden. The repercussions that he had feared regarding his intrusive visit to his dear sister were now manifesting. *Didn't take a prophet for this one,* he thought. On the telephone, Sister Snowden appeared to be very angry and had requested a prompt and private meeting with him. It seemed that there were some difficulties with her suitor, Fellyard Beedley.

The knock on the door signaled to Reverend Sydney that speculation was about to meet reality. Sister Snowden entered the study with her jawbones clenched. To her credit she politely shook Reverend Sydney's hand.

"Good afternoon, Sister Snowden."

"Yes."

Reverend Sydney got the message: no preliminary small talk. He gestured for her to have a seat.

It was a difficult conversation. Sister Snowden frequently switched from one who required comforting to one that tersely chastised the reverend for meddling in her private affairs. Mr. Beedley had informed her that things had changed in his own life and he would now have to concentrate on his other affairs. Sister Snowden took this as Beedley's way of saying that he was tired of her company, or that he did not want to get mixed up with the Reverend Sydney and his Holy Ghost posse.

"Just what did you all say to him?" she said.

"Sister Snowden, we said nothing that would chase him or anyone else away. I was very clear on the fact that we were only concerned for you. If there were no issues, and we didn't think that there were any, then all was well." He was uncomfortable with the way she was looking at him.

"Mr. Beedley himself stated that he understood that our visit only demonstrated our love for you. He said that he recognized that it was not a personal statement of any problems against him. The visit appeared to end on a good note. Did he say anything in particular about our visit?"

"Well, no, not exactly. He did say that it was a good visit and that the conversation was cordial. I then asked him if he would like to join me this Sunday as my personal guest for church services."

Sister Snowden paused as she mentally reconstructed the conversation and how it first seemed all right, that all was fine. Then she could tell that it really did bother him. Her voice went to a whisper, almost pleading to the reverend.

"He gave me a look, Reverend Sydney, like I had said something that was bad. But I had mentioned it before and it seemed to be fine. It was like he had just really thought about it and the thought of it all was twisting him up inside. I just asked him would this Sunday be all right and he gave me such a look. His eyes seemed to change. Very slowly he asked me was there need for such a rush. I tells him that I'm not rushing anything, just suggesting things. He then starts to coughing. Not like he's sick, but kinda like something tasting bad on his tongue." Sister Snowden's emotions then reverted back to one in need of comfort.

"Reverend, he then spits something out on the end of the sleeve and just rolls up his sleeve to cover it. I'm just looking at him, but he is not even acknowledging me, reverend. It's like I'm not even there, like I don't matter."

Reverend Sydney remained still—not looking at Sister Snowden—his eyes drawn to the wooden crucifix that was mounted near the study's window. For some reason it appeared to be the only place that might yield an answer. With reddened eyes blurred from a rush of tears, Sister Snowden did not even notice the reverend's gaze. She continued the tale of her encounter.

"Then he turns to look at me, reverend, but not with the caring eyes that he used to have, but from someone else's, from somewhere else. I don't know this man. He then starts to tell me that the only reason that I want him to come to church is so I can have something to blab about to my church club." A tear dripped from her cheek. "The man then starts on about how I must be telling our business because you asked him about Sister Pearson. He saying that he told me about telling our business, that things between us was just between us. I didn't think that telling you about his interest in Sister Pearson, a fellow church member, was a secret. I only thought that he meant don't say nothing about how often he visits me or where we go."

Reverend Sydney was curious. He kept his head still, his face without expression.

"Mentioning Sister Pearson to you, what's private about that?" The good reverend fully understood that nothing was wrong or private about Sister Snowden's inquiry. He recognized Beedley's comments for what they were: Beedley's privacy argument was a wonderfully ambiguous and convenient excuse to engage in debate, an oft-used camouflage for total disengagement. Reverend Sydney wisely held his assessment as only a thought. He slid his chair from its intended position and moved to be closer to Sister Snowden.

"My dear Sister Snowden, I know that you believe that I am the cause of your fallout with Fellyard Beedley. I also know that part of you understands that something is most certainly not right with what happened, that it really did not have a lot to do with me. I'm not here to browbeat you or to attempt to convince you of my own innocence, that doesn't matter. What is important is that you understand that someone who once expressed a lot of feelings for you has now allowed an innocent inquiry on your part to be the cause of an ugly problem." Reverend Sydney touched her arm to comfort her. "Who knows, he may be sitting home right now trying to formulate an apology to you. If he cares, he will. If not, then you have to affirm your own rationale. I will not attempt to sway you."

Sister Snowden's head remained down as her intelligence gave increased insight to her emotions. The past few weeks had been so special for her. It had been years since she had enjoyed the company of a man who was interested in her attentions. Fellyard

Beedley had seemed so friendly and knowledgeable. He was a man that did not seemed encumbered by financial or health issues; he had reminded Sister Snowden of years gone by, when many a man vied for the attention of the buxom woman from Boston. He slowly reeled in the now silver-haired church member who had allowed time and superb baking skills to alter her silhouette.

Reverend Sydney did not rush his comments. "I really appreciate that you came directly to me with this concern, Sister Snowden. Even if with some anger, it's the only way to address it. I do ask that perhaps you consider continuing this dialogue with one of the sisters of the church. This discussion is profoundly confidential, but sometime there are matters that are best addressed with those of the same gender. I don't even need to know who it is, and I certainly won't be asking how it went. Everything ain't my business. What I will suggest is that you find someone whose ears are not perpetually connected to her mouth. This is your business and what you decide to share should not find its way back into the church, especially before you get there."

Sister Snowden gave him a tired smile. "Thank you, reverend, I'll consider that. Thank you for listening and even allowing me to be angry. You know that I don't hate you."

"My dear sister, the thought never entered my mind. We're saved, but we're still human; we continue to feel pain."

"But still, I was a little warm with you. That was wrong and I apologize."

"Apologize for what, Sister Snowden? I've already forgotten about what may or may not have occurred while two good friends were talking. Memories are a fine thing, sister, but if we don't know when to deny them, then this Christian walk is all a farce." Reverend Sydney frowned and raised an eyebrow toward Sister Snowden. "The only thing that will make your pastor's spirit rise in anger is if he has to wait another Sunday before a certain sister brings in her signature sweet potato pie. You know, complete with that flaky, buttery crust that melts when it even gets close to the tongue. Now that's a sin."

Sister Snowden's face brightened a notch. "Now, reverend, I thought that you told the congregation that you were monitoring your cholesterol and such."

"Ah, don't worry, my dear sister. I'm working on a special cholesterol and reduce-the-calories prayer that will cover such delicacies. If the Father can take five loaves and two fishes and feed thousands, why can't he take one pie and remove the fat?" Sister Snowden laughed as she got up to leave the pastoral study. She appreciated the way that the reverend had allowed a tense meeting to be concluded on a cordial note. "Goodbye, reverend, and thank you," she said. "I'm still a bit confused, but I do feel better."

"You're very welcome, Sister Snowden. You have a very pleasant and blessed day."

"I shall try reverend; of course, I now have some extra things in the kitchen." She turned to look at the reverend.

"But then again, perhaps, I should wait until you finish that prayer, don't want to try God."

"Oh no, Sister, don't you wait for my prayer. You go ahead and fire up that oven! I plan on doing some extra Holy Ghost shouting this Sunday anyway, burns more calories than Tae Bo!"

CHAPTER **THIRTY-ONE**

Toomers spotted the Dodge Ram truck. He pushed LeDain from the driver's door to the passenger's side, reaching over and fastening the boy snugly into his seat belt.

"Can't be having an accident, can we now?" He made sure the belt was taut across the boy's shoulder, then he stroked the back of his hand across LeDain's left cheek.

"Don't worry, we'll be fine, just fine. Wouldn't hurt you for the world, my LeDain. Just keep doing like I say and it'll be a fine weekend." Toomers smiled as he looked at the gas gauge that read full. Good, should be no reason to stop, he thought.

LeDain kept his eyes straight ahead. He was struggling to figure out a way for the nightmare to end without causing harm to himself or his mother. For well over an hour, his reddened eyes monitored the highway traffic. The darkened road and perforated line down the center served to draw his eyes inward, inviting him into a deepened slumber. LeDain did not awaken until he felt a heavy jerk from the turning truck. Toomers had left the highway and was now on the streets of Philadelphia—home.

LeDain was not familiar with this particular area of the city. He believed it to be near the city's south side, yet it was away from any main corridor. He was no stranger to the inner city, but as the truck drove toward a block of dilapidated houses, he realized that this was actually not a real neighborhood. There was no street activity whatsoever. No nocturnal merchants peddling their various wares. Be it illicit pharmaceuticals or twenty-minute sexual escapades, no one was available. No late-night, self-appointed DJs were heard blaring music from oversized car speakers, nor were there any stray mongrels scrounging for marginally edible litter. It was a ghost town within a ghost town. As the truck drove deeper into the housing graveyard, LeDain noticed construction equipment secured within a newly erected chain-link fence. The fence, with its shiny aluminum posts, appeared to lovingly wrap itself around the brand new backhoe and MiniCat. It rendered a perverse message regarding the availability of funds to demolish a community, but never the budget to salvage one. Most understood that it was a never about the lack of funds; rather, it was the dearth of governmental social integrity. The crisis of a terminally ill neighborhood will rarely change the course of those who have resolved to abort its deformed problem. Instead, the social overseers were seeking a new birth in a perfect world of condos and Starbucks.

Toomers turned the lights off on the truck as he looked around for a security sedan. Earlier in the week he had paid a visit to the construction site, gaining access to one of the distant fossilized homes. Toomers knew that the inner-city demolition process would not be a rapid event. Why throw money away by doing it too fast? Far too many palms required their respective blessings.

It was now 5:40 in the morning. The security officer would not be making his last rounds until about 7:30am, just near quitting time. Toomers knew that he could usually count on the fact that many security types believed that if something were to happen, it would be in the late evening or early morning. Few criminals were going to start a task at five in the morning. He had no clue regarding the discovery of the Negro burial site, nor was he aware that construction work would be even slower than normal. He glanced over at LeDain.

"Well, son, we're home." He reached over and unbuckled LeDain from the seat belt. Thoughts of being safe and alone in his getaway haven gave Toomers a new awakening to unnatural senses. All the headaches and deceptive activities of the past few hours would soon be history. He would be alone with the one who often attended his perverse fantasies.

With LeDain in tow, Toomers half-walked, half-ran towards his temporary shelter. Looking around once more, Toomers pushed aside the board on the back door and stepped into the failing brick structure. He produced a small flashlight from his pocket and made his way toward the steps. The stench of garbage and rodent waste did not seem to bother Toomers. He twisted the back of LeDain's shirt and pulled him up the decay-softened stairs. Unshielded rains and boarded windows had served to compromise the house's wooden structures. The stairs were disintegrating to the point where the wrong footstep would send the unsuspecting climber in a different direction. The walls were dark with insects, embedded within a tacky slurp of bird feces and black-green mold.

"Ah, here we are, the presidential suite," said Toomers. He shoved LeDain through the doorway then closed it behind them as if not to disturb others in the house. He had somehow fashioned a makeshift apartment out of a dank bedroom. It contained a military cot, a small folding table, and a camping lantern.

"I know it's not much, but it will do for now." He looked at the trembling LeDain.

"Besides, see what I bought for us?" He pointed to the side wall where on the floor stood a row of six large candles.

"Sometimes it's good to set the mood, you know? It'll be just fine here. Come over here, LeDain." LeDain did not move. He had lost some of his fearfulness and was not going to be a willing participant in whatever the beast in front of him had in mind.

"Come here, I say!" LeDain still did not move.

"Oh, you forgot what I said about your mother, did you? Never mind, I tried to be nice to you, make it nice for both of us but you want to act up." Toomers kept his eyes on LeDain as he kneeled down on the floor. His eyes fixed with a growing hate. He was angry because LeDain was changing the way things had previously played out in Toomers' mind. He reached under the cot and pulled out a small duffel bag. A smile formed on his face knowing that LeDain was ignorant of its contents. Any emotional change or increase in intensity served to heighten the lustful anticipation of the deranged professor.

"Let's just see what we have for my precious-precious." Toomers reached into the bag and took out a roll of duct tape and black-lens goggles.

"You don't mind if we do a little role-play?" LeDain looked towards the window and the door, seeking any opening.

As Toomers started towards the frightened young man, he noticed that a bit of light was coming through a crack in the window's boarding.

"Damn. Sun's coming up." The professor was full with desire, yet he didn't want the daylight to ruin what he thought would be an encounter best savored by night. Too many variables came into play during the day: the increased possibility of construction personnel or security showing up. It was Friday and who knows who might decide to show up today? Seeing that Toomers was momentarily distracted, LeDain made a quick dash towards the door. Toomers was quicker than his jellied frame implied. In three quick leaps he caught LeDain and slammed him against the wall. Toomers then pulled the child towards his body. He twisted LeDain around until his right arm encircled the chest of the young man. Sensing the beginning of a scream, Toomers placed his left hand over LeDain's mouth. For a moment Toomers said nothing, perversely savoring the moment, the closeness of two deep-breathing bodies.

"Oh, not now, not now, young LeDain," mocked Toomers. "Oh how I wish it were so, don't you? We'll have to wait for later on. Right now I'm going to have to use my good friend Mr. Duct Tape here to keep watch over you. Don't worry, I'll be back soon. Daddy has to run a few errands now. Gotta get rid of the monster truck out there. It's a tad too obvious in this area." Toomers cocked his head to the side, uncertain if the whispers were returning. He held the struggling boy down while unceremoniously wrapping duct tape around his mouth, finishing with his hands. He then reached in the bag to retrieve a rope, using it to secure LeDain to an old radiator.

"You got enough room to lie down on that cot. I tied your hands in front in case you need to use that pot over there. Don't worry if you miss, the maid will be in soon to clean it up." He chuckled. "Sorry I can't trust you without the duct tape. I'll be back in a couple of hours with something to eat. The best thing for you to do is to just relax. You'll find that I'm all right, that we'll like each other for a long time." LeDain had stopped crying: in place of his tears was the look of a boy who was summoning manhood.

He glared at Toomers as if daring him to remove the bindings. The scared little boy was no longer at home. In its place was a young man who would use any available weapon to overcome the professor turned psychopath. It was a look that gave pause to the professor. He took one last look at the boy. LeDain appeared to be losing the tantalizing spice of innocence that served to season Toomers' cravings. He threw the duct tape to the floor and stormed out of the room.

CHAPTER **THIRTY-TWO**

Silent tears returned to LeDain's cheeks as he heard the steps of his professor begin to fade in the distance. Thoughts moved in pinball fashion as visions of his mother and memories of his brother joined recollections of classroom activities at New Passage Academy. His jaw tightened against quivering lips as he struggled to control his bodily functions. Although a previous resident of a hostile concrete neighborhood, LeDain had yet to don the hardened veneer of a survival-minded child. The loving protection of his older brother, Jared, had shielded him from the fury of the streets.

LeDain's small frame had already begun to cramp from sitting in one position. He sniffed a few more times as his thoughts returned once more to Jared and his brotherly strength. *I'll be strong for myself now Jared.* His cheeks began to dry as he looked about the unfriendly room, determined to change his situation—to at least try. LeDain's heart leaped. Creaking wood told him that the professor had decided to forgo his trip and return to torment his young hostage. His muscles dared not move as the rigid boy continued to listen; again hearing movement in the splintered beams. His leg pulled on the thick rope, futilely willing it to release its captive. Firmly bound wrists offered no opportunity for escape. Fear continued to work its cruel magic, subconsciously giving orders to his lungs not to breathe. It took another moment for LeDain to understand that it was only the noise from an old house that lamented its prolonged exposure to the elements. Warped and tired wood, still bound by nails and metal restraints, occasionally yawned in protest. The young boy allowed his shoulders to relax as he leaned back against the grimy wall.

Breathing had just returned to an almost normal rhythm when he realized that he was indeed being watched. Black marbled eyes peered at him from the left side of a once blue coffee can that lay on its dented side. At first, LeDain believed that his

145

senses were again toying with his mind. A flickering movement from the marbles gave the young captive sight of the steel wool coat of an aging rodent. For a moment, both held the other's gaze. Then, from the corner of his eye, LeDain caught the movement of a small pile of rags that lay bunched on the other side of the discolored radiator.

Just how many are in this place? thought LeDain as his skin began to prickle. The old rat's eyes rolled slightly toward the rag pile but swiftly returned toward the direction of the odd-looking stranger. It was as if the rat was used to the presence of humans. In the past, the rodent would simply slink away and wait for any humans to leave. But terms were different now, the rat was used to empty premises. It was the human's turn to scamper away.

LeDain was tempted to kick at the scraggly rodent but feeling the tension from the rope, decided against it. After all, the situation was only a staring contest and he had other problems to deal with. LeDain almost laughed to himself as he realized that the arrival of the disturbing critter had allowed a brief respite from his earlier fears and anxieties. He still had to find a way to quickly get out of room, the housing area, before the real rat returned. Sheltered by his brother or not, LeDain was still very aware of the perverse appetites that afflicted many adults, especially towards children. He ventured one more look toward his ragged roommate. It was gone. Looking out of his window, LeDain could tell that time was moving on. He had to find some way to escape. Soon, the only sounds that could now be heard were the thuds that came from the back of his head as it repeatedly hit the flaking wall. *Think LeDain, think think.*

CHAPTER THIRTY-THREE

Synthia Pearson sat in the waiting area of the police station. In her hands was the note that LeDain had slipped her. She also had the folder of information on the academy that she had received from Mrs. Matthews.

"Mrs. Pearson?" a tall man said.

"Yes, I'm Mrs. Pearson." Synthia stood up.

"Hello, my name is Detective Christian Tunnell. We spoke on the phone."

"Pleased to meet you, Detective Tunnell. I'm glad that you could see me."

"From what you've told me over the phone it sounds like we have to address this matter, and quickly. Do you have the note with you?" Synthia handed LeDain's note to the detective. The detective politely took the note and pulled up a chair alongside Synthia and began to read: Seen you on the TV before. *You like to help people. This is a great place, but one of the teachers makes me scared. Nobody's listening now; it's very hard to call my mother. Don't know how long I can keep him away from me. I think that he likes children. My mother's name is Nora Sanford, from Philly. Help me! LeDain Sanford.*

"You say that you got this from a private school?" said Detective Tunnell.

"Yes, the school is called New Passage Academy."

"Hmm, don't think that I've heard of it," he said. "Where is it located?"

"It's in Maryland, and no, you wouldn't have heard of it." She briefly shared the story of New Passage.

"You're kidding me, right? A private school for ghetto kids and no one knows anything about it? Come on, stop pulling my leg."

"No, I'm afraid it is true, Detective Tunnell. But think about it. One of the reasons that it might remain secretive is the fact that no one expects for there to be an academic school for those of color. The other difficulty may be the fact that it is funded by people of the black community." She thought about the conversation she and Chadric had in their kitchen. "Let's be honest, all these factors are not the usual expectation, so therefore it makes it easy for people not to see it. Tell me, detective, how many times have you been on an undercover assignment and a bust was just about to go down. Be honest, your first personal directive was to ensure that your fellow officers, white or black, understood that you were indeed a police officer. You wanted to make certain that no black-equals-bad thoughts manifested into an oops." She let what she had said sink in. "Yes, detective, you understand that we sometimes see before we look. You appear incredulous regarding the existence of an extremely private, academic facility for those of color. What if I told you that this was a Jewish school? Your response would be something like: Oh yeah, they got it like that, am I wrong?"

Detective Tunnell smiled. He didn't argue the point. "Okay, you got me. Guilty as charged. Back to the boy: what do you make of it? You sure that he's just not trying to get back home? As bad as abuse is some kids have learned to use this volatile issue to manipulate things for their own agenda. We even had one little girl cry wolf because a male teacher had given her a bad grade."

"I understand, but I don't think that this is the case," said Synthia. "His body language as well as his eyes spoke to me of sincerity."

"You're telling me that the children cannot leave this place and that they are essentially academic hostages?"

"That is not the place as I understand it, nor as I believe it to be. But, as with anything, there are exceptions," said Synthia. "I met and conversed with a few of the children. I do not believe them to be that great a collection of actors that they could fool me with false contentment. I'm of the belief that, perhaps, certain policies, specific to student liberties are changing or have changed." She gave a worried look to Detective Tunnell. "Detective, I want to be certain that neither LeDain nor any other child is in any personal danger. When I spoke to one of the educators at the school, he shared that a few administrative items have shifted. It also appears that he does not hold agreement with these changes."

Detective Tunnell stood up. "Mrs. Pearson, I need names and contact numbers. It's time to move."

Detective Tunnell sat on his living-room couch, beer in hand. Today the television was watching him. He was waiting to hear from his contact at the Maryland police station. Earlier the detective had forwarded the particulars of the case and was informed that a Detective Eisner would be the responding authority.

Detective Tunnell shared a rare evening meal with his wife and three children. He watched the children a little closer this evening. He listened to each of them share their spectacular event of the day: the most exciting involved a frog and a cracked specimen jar. He smiled. He enjoyed the fact that the most adventurous occurrence in his children's lives involved a leaking frog. His mind drifted to the probability of a private academy for inner-city children. He fully understood the need to address any problems that involved the well-being of children. What also held his thought was the question regarding any need for such an academic project. Just as he had reflected on the wonderful innocence of the life of his children, there were thousands whose highlight of day might be another shooting or gang recruitment attempt. He also reflected on the young Christian Tunnell.

As a thirteen-year-old boy, Detective Tunnell had great aspirations to become an engineer. His struggle with mathematics did not dissuade him from his decision. Part of the problem was that no one in his family had ever attended college; therefore, there were few to guide the young boy. Time went on and his struggles continued. He tried hard but few of his teachers saw enough in him to support his academic quest. As middle school turned into high school, his encouragement came in the form of collective disinterest. Christian was now caught in the quandary of being an inner-city, public-school, middle-class citizen. In a system of overcrowded classes with frequent school disruptions and a non-stop turnstile on the teacher's lounge door, the middle-class student was embraced. In some schools they were the invisible wave of nameless backpacks that received a quick pat on the head literally as they passed by. No one had great expectations for them; some people even discouraged them when they dared to reveal any traits of ambition. All available resources were budgeted for the diamonds or the 'n'er do wells'. Many schools failed to realize that diamonds exist in many forms, that the crudest rock when handled properly can produce an astonishing gem.

Christian Tunnell never did get the opportunity to attend college. Sporadic and low-paying jobs eventually led the motivated young man to the police academy where he breezed through the academic rigors of the course. It wasn't that he was bitter. He had done well for himself as a police officer and a detective. He and his wife worked hard—saved harder—and managed to purchase a home in a quiet area of the metropolitan Philadelphia. Christian Tunnell did not believe that life had dealt him a disabling tragedy, especially compared to many of his classmates. What did occasionally bother him was the fact that he never received the chance to pursue the dreams of a young man. What was lacking in his spirit was the fact that the aspiring engineer was never allowed an honest opportunity to fail.

"Are you just gonna let that ring?" Lana his wife said, standing near the sofa with her hands on her round hips.

"Huh?" Detective Tunnell blinked the apple of his eye into focus.

"*Huh?* the phone, Detective Holmes. C'mon, get on the case!" She teased.

"All right, Miss Got-After-Dinner-Jokes."

He noted the Caller ID, Maryland.

"Hello, this is Detective Tunnell."

"Good evening, detective. This is Detective Eisner, Maryland Police."

"Yes, thank you for getting back to me, Detective Eisner. What can you tell me?"

"Not a whole hell of a lot, which also raises my personal antennae."

"Tell me, Eisner, this academy, is it news to you?" There was a brief pause on the other end.

"No, not exactly, detective. We've been cordial neighbors with New Passage Academy for years. We've never had any problems and when we do see anyone, they are polite and respectable to a fault. Nevertheless, a matter regarding the safety of a child still takes precedent over neighborly goodwill."

"I'm glad to hear you say that, Detective Eisner."

"Oh, what did you expect, some leave-us-alone-you-uppity-northerner-type response? You thinking that I sit on the hood of my rusty cruiser playing the theme from *Deliverance?*"

"Oh no, nothing like—"

"Relax, Tunnell, just messing with you. No, the law is the law and nothing comes before a child's welfare. I've already been in contact with New Passage Academy and have made plans to pay them a visit in the morning. I'll also make sure that I spend some time speaking with the child in question."

"Just when are you going, detective?"

"I plan on taking the ferry over tomorrow at about ten in the morning: care to ride?"

"Would love to, and thanks for the invite."

"I know that you're not around the corner and the hour is late, but I had a feeling that you'd want to see things firsthand."

"It's okay, I'll sleep next week. I'll be taking the train down and then get a rental car and drive to your precinct."

"Sounds good, we'll be looking out for you."

Detective Tunnell hung up the telephone and walked into the bedroom to speak with his wife. She understood her husband's heart and need to extend himself regarding this particular case.

"What time are you leaving?" she said.

"Oh, probably about 3:30 in the morning."

"You go take a shower and put your head down for little bit. I'll pack an overnight bag just in case." They both looked at each other, agreeing in silence that the well-being of a child was indeed the priority. Both Christian and his wife often spoke of how those who are blessed should also stand in humble obligation to those less fortunate. They frequently reminded their children that extending themselves to others is for the most part only a temporary inconvenience.

Detective Tunnell set his clock for 2:45 in the morning and prepared to take a shower. He passed by the bedroom of his sleeping children and smiled upward.

CHAPTER **THIRTY-FOUR**

Detectives Eisner and Tunnell were on board New Passage Academy's luxury ferry. They tried their best to be as nonchalant as possible as they surveyed the expensive décor of the shuttle vessel.

Seaman Willie Smallfort informed the detectives that they'd soon be getting underway. He also told him that the ferry's captain would be returning soon from his postal errand.

"Seems like Captain Meeks decided to stay on board last night. Told me that he had forgotten about a package that he had promised to send to his grandchildren. You know how it is with grandpas," said Seaman Smallfort. "He could have simply sent one of us to take care of that matter. Even volunteered myself, I know all kinds of shortcuts to the post office. But I guess it seems more special when you actually send it off yourself."

"It's quite all right," said Detective Eisner.

"I'm sure that he'll be back shortly."

"Oh, yes, ma'am… I mean, detective. He'll be back real soon. Anything I can get you, I mean you two?" said Smallfort. Detective Eisner was modestly dressed, but it still did not hide the fact that she was quite a stunning woman. Her large eyes gently angled toward high cheekbones covered by smooth, olive skin.

"No, we're fine. Thank you, Mr. Smallfort," she said." Smoothing his hair down, Smallfort left the detectives to address other ship needs. Detective Tunnell grinned. He observed the obvious infatuation of the young ferry seaman. He looked out of one of the ferry's windows and saw Captain Meeks making his way toward the gangplank.

"Looks like we'll be leaving soon. I do believe that the captain is on his way."

"Great," said Detective Eisner. "Let me make a call to New Passage Academy to confirm our ETA and contact person." She opened her mobile phone and began to dial the number of the Academy. Detective Tunnell turned toward the leather recliners to continue his private awe-inspiring inspection. "What do you mean, they're not there? Just where are they?" Detective Eisner got a bad feeling. Tunnell whipped his head around towards Detective Eisner. Neither his mind nor his heart liked the sound of her voice. He paused for a moment, noticing that the ferry was moving. The captain appreciated his tardiness and upon boarding had immediately made his way to the bridge to initiate launching procedures. "What's wrong, Eisner?" said Detective Tunnell.

"Who's not there?" Eisner stared at her fellow detective. "It's LeDain, they can't seem to find him. It gets worse: one of the professors is also gone."

"Who is this professor?" Detective Tunnell came down with a dose of bad feeling too.

"His name is Toomers, Brodrey Toomers." Tunnell pointed toward the cell phone.

"Are they still on the line? When did they last see them?" He quickly stopped speaking, a sheepish look on his face. "I'm sorry, detective. I'm spouting off like you don't know your job, forgive me."

Detective Eisner smiled at Detective Tunnell. "Don't worry, Tunnell, ain't thin-skinned over it. Tell you what: I'll get more information while you call in an Amber Alert. When we get to the academy, we'll find out more. Professor Toomers has a home on the island. We'll head there first. It won't take us long to get there. I'll also radio in for the helicopter to be on standby as well as the hostage team. This way all will be ready if needed."

"Will do," said Tunnell. "Like I said, sorry for being in the way of a detective doing her job."

"Oh, shut up, you," said Eisner. "We're on the same team." Her voice softened, "We'll find him." Tunnell made the

Amber Alert call and watched as the speed of the ferry increased. Suddenly the door opened and in walked the ferry's captain.

"Why hello, detectives. Captain Meeks at your service. Heard that you need to get to the academy on important business. That's why I got started before I stuck my head in to bid proper greetings."

"That's quite all right, Captain Meeks. Yes, we do need to be off. It seems that there may be some form of trouble at the academy, we need to get there as soon as possible if you don't mind." The expression on the Captain's face immediately changed. He took the walkie-talkie unit from his belt and promptly issued orders for maximum speed to Cushsons Island.

"Thank you, Captain," said Detective Eisner.

"Don't mention it, detective, just sorry that I wasn't here earlier. Stayed on the ferry last night and forgot that I had an errand to run."

"You usually spend the night on board, Captain?" said Detective Tunnell. "I will say that, after looking at this vessel, I ain't particularly mad at you."

"Yes, she is a fine vessel. But last night I had a call from the academy for an emergency pickup. Seems like a young lad has yet to get over the death of his big brother. One of the teachers was taking him home."

Captain Meeks stopped talking. He noticed that both detectives were moving toward him, their faces paling.

"What... what's wrong?"

"Did you get the boy's name?" asked Eisner.

"Did he personally speak to you?" said Tunnell.

"Well I... no, he didn't say a word. Professor Toomers did all the talking. He's the one who told me about the lad's troubles. He said that the boy was too upset."

"Did the boy look all right? Did he look harmed?" said Detective Eisner.

"He was kinda quiet, sitting by himself, but he seemed okay."

"Think carefully, captain. Did the professor say where he was headed?" said Detective Tunnell.

"I really can't recall, but I do know that the lad was from Philadelphia." Captain Meeks froze, all color emptied from his sea-worn face. "Oh shit! Is that the trouble that you all are talking about? Now that everything comes back to me, it all seems to fit! Was he taking that boy and I helped? I even gave him the keys to my truck!"

"Please, captain," said Detective Eisner, "turn this ferry around now! We've got to get back!" Captain Meeks was already on the walkie-talkie barking orders for a high-speed return to the dock. Detective Eisner called back to her precinct while Tunnell did the same with his.

"Captain Meeks," yelled Tunnell, "I need a description of your truck!"

"It's a black Dodge Ram truck. By the way it has a GPS system. You should be able to track it without problem."

"Finally, good news," said Eisner as she looked at Tunnell. She made another call to New Passage Academy to convey that Professor Toomers had left the island with LeDain Sanford. She let them know that all of Toomers' personnel files were to be immediately faxed to the police station. She also informed them that a helicopter and an investigation team would be making their way to the island and staff and student interviews would begin this afternoon. No sooner than Eisner had gotten off the phone, Detective Tunnell's cell phone rang.

"This is Detective Tunnell. What do you have for me?" He listened to the caller. "Okay, great. Keep me posted. I should be there this afternoon. No, I'm going to find a nearby airport, gotta be some way to get to Philadelphia in short order." He glanced toward a nodding Eisner. "Yes, I will be there this afternoon. Let me know when someone's physically at the truck." He hung up the phone and gave a tight-jawed nod to Eisner.

"They've tracked down the truck and a unit is on its way to check it out. Because of its location they think that the truck has been abandoned, but we'll know pretty soon." He looked over at Detective Eisner and Captain Meeks.

"I don't think that he would take the boy all the way to Philadelphia only to do him immediate harm."

"Yes, but we don't know if he panicked, or if he has done anything on the way to Philadelphia. Sorry, don't mean to sound so negative about things. I'm just trying to cover all of the bases." Detective Eisner jotted down some notes.

"No, you're right," said Tunnell. "We do have to consider all of the possibilities." Captain Meeks had moved to a corner chair, almost collapsing in an upright heap.

Eisner walked over to the dejected captain. "Captain, you do know that it is not your fault. How were you to know, how was anyone to know?"

Meeks looked up with red eyes. "I gave that bastard the keys to my truck, just put a ribbon on things for him."

"Yes, captain, but that ribbon allowed us to quickly determine his whereabouts. We'll soon be finding them both; not in spite of, but thanks to you." Detective Eisner looked out of the window.

"Looks like we'll soon be at the dock, Captain Meeks. We'll keep you posted on things; in the meantime here's my card. If anyone from the academy makes a request to leave the island, please give me a call." Captain Meeks' hair now appeared more gray than white. He took the card from the detective and left to prepare for docking. Tunnell watched the man as he left.

"Poor guy. He'll be beating himself up for a long time. I need to get back to Philadelphia as soon as possible."

"Don't worry, we'll set up a charter flight for you; you'll be back home by 1:30pm."

"Thanks, Eisner, I really appreciate it."

"Call me Caroline. This reason is as good as any to spend some of that emergency budget money. I'll keep you posted on what's going on with the investigation from this end. Be sure to let me know how things are going in Philadelphia."

"Count on it. By the way, the name's Christian."

Detective Eisner smiled. "Let's pray that this one has a good ending, Detective Christian."

"I'll join you in that prayer, Detective Caroline."

CHAPTER THIRTY-FIVE

It was 1:10 in the morning. Reverend Sydney was alone in his home study. His wife, Darmela Sydney, in her ambitious quest for new solo material, had long finished her perusal of the church hymnals. After a 10:30pm rehearsal of *God Can Do Anything,* she had retired for the night. Relieved that the coast was clear, Sam, their golden retriever, made his way back from his sanctuary in the laundry room. He trampled by Reverend Sydney's study and gave what the reverend swore was a look of concern and headed toward his sleeping rug.

"Sorry Sam," whispered the reverend. *Just pray that God grants her either a voice or an ear.* Reverend Sydney had intended to get some additional work done on this coming Sunday's sermon. He believed that he had the template. He just could not focus on how to deliver the message. With a Bible in front of him, he pressed himself to get motivated for study. Initially, it was the business of the church that distracted him. The day had been long with the usual duties that presented itself to a full-time pastor. The monthly billing statements of the church were confirmed, all was current and in order. There had been several discussions throughout the day with Deacon Bazemore regarding the roofing project and contract specifics. Reverend Sydney began to believe that he had locked in on how he wanted to format the sermon when the day's meeting with Sister Snowden came to mind. His thoughts then immediately leaped to her friend Fellyard Beedley.

Overall, Reverend Sydney was pleased regarding the meeting, especially how it had ended in an upbeat fashion. Sister Snowden would be all right, he thought. It may take a little time, but she would be fine. He was also privately pleased that Mr. Beedley appeared to be out of her life, that a visit from the church—albeit non-threatening—had been enough to dissuade any future manipulative attempts. He understood the Sister Snowden remained upset but he'd rather she was upset regarding losing her special friend then eventually losing so much more. Reverend Sydney lifted his head to the ceiling. "Thank you, Jesus."

To temporarily suspend all church matters from his mind, and more importantly any disturbing issues, Reverend Sydney decided to take a break and continue his plans for his upcoming family visit. He and his wife had been making plans to visit his brother, Garry Sydney, in Houston, Texas. Garry Sydney was also a pastor and had recently built a church in the Houston area. For months, Reverend Garry Sydney had begged his brother to come and pay him and his congregation a visit. The two brothers would get some fishing and Reverend Sydney would get an opportunity to deliver the two Sunday morning services at Greater Cathedral in Christ. Reverend Sydney turned on his computer and went now online to look up things to do in Houston. He knew that his brother would show him around but sibling rivalry never changed. Reverend Sydney wanted to surprise his brother by already being in the know.

Quickly growing bored with surfing the web, Reverend Sydney decided to locate his brother's church using the online map service, complete with satellite imagery. He was astounded by the aerial and hybrid views that were available to him on the web. Not only was he able to find the church, but he was almost able to see where the pastoral parking space was located. He was just getting ready to logoff and return his focus to his sermon when a thought hit him: since he was playing with the map service, perhaps, he could locate his own church; see how it looked from above.

As he reached toward the keyboard to type in the address of his church, he was instead compelled to enter the address of Fellyard Beedley. An unsteady drumming exploded in Reverend Sydney's own chest as he typed in the address. *Why's my breathing all off?* he thought. It's just an address. He paused before he pressed the 'Enter' key. The map service revealed two possible locations for his search. Reverend Sydney's first inclination was to use this delay as an excuse to exit the map website. He denied the inclination; curiosity remained an insatiable beast. Selecting the appropriate address, he again pressed 'Enter'. The monitor quickly changed to reveal the location of Felton Beedley's home.

With courage renewed, Reverend Sydney accessed the satellite view. Immediately the aerial view of Felton Beedley's home was on the screen.

"No problem," said Reverend Sydney. "All appears to be in order." He smiled at himself for becoming so caught up in things.

"Look at you," he said, "A man of God no less." As he reached to logoff, his eyes moved to the satellite view area outside the house. What was wrong? The details leaped from the monitor and into his spirit. The lawn ornaments. On the ground, the assembly was an innocuous arrangement. From the air, the wooden orbs and planks gave detail to a form that more than hinted of a crude pentagram. The revelation soared through Reverend Sydney in both body and spirit. Even if he were jumping to conclusions, his very being had already been irrecoverably convinced. He turned off the computer and remained seated at his desk. His eyes found the Bible and he pulled it towards his chest. The drumming in his heart subsided, saliva returned to his tongue as he became more and more comforted by the physical connection to The Word. Not one for religious hysterics, he was aware that there were indeed forces in the world that claimed no home in this world. He didn't realize when he had started but he found himself in the midst of a prayer.

The shrill of the telephone interrupted his earnest communion with the Father. Reverend Sydney took another look at the clock: 1:35am. *Who would be calling at this hour?* He attempted to recall if any of his parishioners were in grave health. As a pastor of a mid-sized congregation, he understood that there were a variety of needs that might dictate a late call. He had twice been in the emergency room that year and had also journeyed to the police station to support the bail process of a church member's nephew. He reached to pick up the receiver and hesitated. He wasn't sure why he paused, but he was sensing something that did not coincide with the usual pastorals summons.

"Oh please, Reverend," he said to himself. "I do believe that your upcoming vacation will get here soon." He picked up the telephone and began to say hello when the voice on the other end leaped right in.

"Good morning, Reverend Sydney," said a raspy voice. "I trust that I did not awaken you, but something tells me that you are not in your bed. A reverend's work is never done, is it?"

"Mr. Beedley, good morning." Reverend Sydney knew there was no denying the evidence of his voice or his presence.

"Oh, so you know who this is?"

"Yes, I know you."

"I was just calling to let you know that there are no hard feelings. I know that Quentella Snowden must have told you by now that things are a little different between us. What can I say? I guess I'm just too mobile a man to stay still for long. Got to get around, you know?"

"Yes, I know, Mr. Beedley. It's probably for the best that things have changed. I'm certain that both of you shall find appropriate, or good company elsewhere."

"Yeah, I probably will, always have. Did you just insult me, reverend?"

"No insult intended, Mr. Beedley. We are all better matched within our own respective circles. By the way, did you ever get the chance to meet with the journalist Synthia Pearson?" There was a vacuum-like hesitation on the other end of the phone.

"No, we didn't. I guess that we are both very busy with other matters. I believe that I will have one of my associates make contact with the lady. That should work out just as well."

Reverend Sydney paused. "Then I need not speak with her regarding a meeting? All matters with my church members are settled?"

"No meeting necessary. I'm sure that as an anchorwoman and all, she would be too tied up with reporting concerning the city. Besides, I hear that she's currently on a very special school project. School's more important: gotta checkup on the tender little ones."

"Why did you really call me, Mr. Beedley?"

"Well, Reverend Sydney, since you and your church paid me a friendly visit, I merely wanted to return the courtesy. You people of the cloth are such a mystery to me. You profess such high spirituality and holiness, but you all seemed so uncomfortable in my home. I just don't understand." Reverend Sydney could almost see Fellyard Beedley's sneer through the phone.

"Yes, Mr. Beedley, it's true. Sometimes the children of God are uncomfortable around certain people. But I do not believe that to be proof of inconsistency but, perhaps, as confirmation of one's truer spiritual position. While being polite, a vegetarian will not sit too long at a table full of meat. Mr. Beedley, I don't know you or your background. You can actually be a most pleasant and cordial man, but your call tonight tells me that perhaps our fears were not unfounded. It is not a statement of judgment. But from your call, from what I've heard today, I feel that I should offer a little prayer on your behalf."

"I don't need your damn prayers!" Fellyard hissed, his voice hard.

"I'm afraid that's one thing that is out of your hands, Mr. Beedley. You're not required to join me or sanction me regarding my prayers to the Father. Perhaps there is some good in the man who welcomed me into his home. I want to pray that that becomes the total man. I'd be more pleased if we could meet at my church office just to chat—" The phone went dead.

CHAPTER **THIRTY-SIX**

The dusted sky gave evidence of only a few stars. Brodrey Toomers hoped that the night would give off enough light for him to make his way back though the construction site without the need of a flashlight. He had ditched the oversized pickup truck and was now on foot. In his haste to return to his temporary dwelling, he had left the food and his flashlight in the truck. His thoughts were centered on LeDain. All other issues were frivolous distractions.

His face no longer resembled that of a distinguished professor. His cheekbones were sunken, deep creases coursed under his blank eyes. Even his gait, once upright and determined, now dragged to one side as if hobbled by ankle restraints. He had managed to secure a pint of cheap whiskey during his shopping excursion. He stopped for a moment to enjoy a draw on the glass flask. Spirits joined with spittle leaked from his mouth and filtered through his gray stubble. His carnal thoughts were focused on LeDain, who remained restrained in his filthy lair. His pace increased as he hastened to act on his lust. Sinful voices implored him to dismiss the minutest thought of returning to sanity. Any feeble whispering of decency that made its way to his mind was quickly subdued by unfulfilled demons. Toomers leaned on the fencing that surrounded the construction site and caught his breath. His left hand was extended above his head, gripping the meshing of the sagging fence. All the while he swayed to the rhythm of a dark symphony. The gray, shrouded moon offered a silhouette of his frame that reminded him of a venomous spider waiting within its web.

Renewing both strength and lust, he pushed himself off of his aluminum recliner and made his way through the loosened earth. He mumbled aloud, fighting the audible demons that joined his journey toward the still boarded houses. He hurried his steps and maneuvered his way around a Porta Potty. A couple of rats scurried past with an unwelcoming glance at the intruder who dared to disturb their desolate sanctuary. In the distance he heard yelling coming from his new abode. *Dammit,* he thought, that boy has somehow worked the gag from his mouth.

Toomers was pretty certain that the boy could not remove his leg restraints and was still tethered to the discolored radiator. Still, it would not do for the yelling to continue. Someone would hear it. He looked around to see if anyone was nearby, especially security personnel. He would have to hurry. Fear and anger propelled him toward the row house. He had to silence the boy. This made him more upset. The thought of doing harm diminished the anticipatory lust that stoked his cravings.

Mentally distracted and focused solely on the house, he failed to notice a metal cart that contained two makeshift coffins. Earlier that day the site's security personnel had come across two sets of remains that had been inadvertently left by the Historical Society. Three transport teams were involved with the project. Each believed that one of the others had made the final trip in removing the last remains. It was almost 7:00 in the evening when the remains were discovered. The men had placed a tarp over the cart to protect it from the elements. The security company decided to wait until the morning to call the assigned funeral parlor. It was not as if any of the bodies needed embalming.

A pink-nosed rat leaped in front of Toomers. He gave an angry but futile kick in its direction. LeDain was yelling again. *Gonna have to shut him up for good I guess,* thought Toomers. *Gotta be some tools on that,* he thought while looking at the metal cart.

Partially lifting up the tarp, he reached underneath to feel for something heavy enough to do a swift job. "What the hell?"

He grabbed something that his mind could not immediately identify. He pulled the object out from under the tarp to reveal a skeletal arm with a hand attached. He and LeDain yelled. His fear caused him to violently twist away from the cart. He simultaneously attempted to toss away the gruesome appendage but somehow only the ulna and radius were tossed. The skeletal hand was snagged on his oversized cuff button. He emitted a rasping scream and flung his arm to get rid of the gritty hand.

His marionette-like movements caused his left foot to slip. He instinctively reached out, grabbing the tarp to break his fall. The force and torque of his falling weight only served to pull the cart down on him, spilling its grisly contents upon his head. His blood chilled over. He stood up and screamed into the night sky as he tried to brush off the dirt and bone fragments. He spun around, planting his right foot in the uneven earth, intent on hurling himself away from the unforeseen horror. He failed to establish good footing and slipped. The force of his intended movement violently propelled him forward and downward. Directly in his downward path was a small stack of concrete chunks. A few of the chunks still had rebar rods protruding from them. He heard one last distant plea from LeDain: a split second before a six-inch rod rammed through his right eye, smoothly settling itself within his already damaged brain. His body twisted and jerked, not convinced of its demise. Twice his back arched as if attempting to dislodge itself from the unyielding rod. His spasmodic finger movements peaked the interest of a very curious rodent. The rat cautiously approached but quickly darted away when a security officer rounded the corner.

The officer aimed his flashlight at Toomers' awkwardly splayed body. His flashlight then rapidly swept toward the houses when he heard the cries of a child. Professor Brodrey Toomers would never know the macabre sight that his body would display to the homicide detectives. The skeletal hand lay across his lifeless face.

Strobe lights and sirens littered the night as Officer Vasquez carried LeDain Sanford from his boarded, dank prison. LeDain's fierce grip around the officer's neck was actually becoming uncomfortable. Officer Vasquez said not a word but held the young boy closer.

Propped against a splintered pole that once carried the communication lines of the telephone and cable companies was a thin, elderly figure wearing a Fedora hat. His arms crossed, obviously displeased. *Brodrey-boy, you were more perverted than I realized, he thought. What good are you to me now? Not only did you get yourself killed, but you also brought a world of* attention *to my academy. The very thing that I was trying to avoid. Now the spotlight is all over the school. All because you couldn't pace yourself, and then you let a bunch of coon skeletons scare you. Them that's gone ain't got no power, most times.*

Fellyard Beedley fixed his hat, sighed, and walked away. He lamented the rapid failure of his plan to implant rot within an unsuspecting host. He turned the corner and melted into the welcoming shadows.

CHAPTER **THIRTY-SEVEN**

"Are these truly the last of the remains?" asked Mr. Conway, a member of the Historical Society, as he placed the bones on an examining table.

"I believe they are," said Abigail Sengal. Abigail Sengal was the head mortician for Sengal Funeral Services. She was also the coordinator for the interment project for the disturbed remains of what was once a Negro cemetery. She was pleased to be a part of such an honorable undertaking. She believed it to be not only her job, but her mission to ensure that the remains of these once-called 'insignificant' people were respectfully relocated. She issued strict instructions for everyone to pay close attention to where the remains were temporarily stored: nothing was to be idly stored in some convenient cardboard box. She was very upset to learn that the last remains had been kept overnight on some construction cart.

"Anything could have gotten to those remains," she told the site foreman. "You most certainly could have called." It did not help matters when she discovered that the remains had been disturbed by the suspected kidnapper. "How the skeletal hand wound up on a new corpse is beyond me. I guess we will never know." She looked down at her last assignment.

"Well, my good fellow," she said to the remains, not caring if Mr. Conway heard her. "Let's get you ready for a proper service, shall we? Hmm, what's this?" She ran a finger along the bone. "Can you please hand me that magnifying glass, Mr. Conway?" Only her humming could be heard in the room. "Don't think that I'm going to call CSI, but this seems like a bullet wound marking on the rib. What irony, to be killed over a century ago and then to be part of a homicide in the new millennium. Ah, Granddaddy used to tell me that there were no accidents, that there is a purpose and meaning to everything."

A piece of crusted metal near the pelvic bone caught Abigail's eye. "What have we here? Seems to be an old belt buckle of some sort. Something's scratched on it." She used a cleansing gauze to remove some of the debris from the buckle. "Mr. Conway, I do believe that our friend here may be trying to introduce himself to us. It's not much, may not even be his, but I'm of the mind that TS has just made his presence known to the twenty-first century." She respectfully placed the belt buckle next to the skeleton. "TS, my friend, I don't know who you are, don't know your story. But I am happy that we have a chance to offer some dignity to someone who was deemed too unworthy to even decay next to others. Hope that this world gave you a little peace in your life." She closed the lid on the metal coffin and whispered to its tenant: "Your work is done, TS. And like my granddaddy would say, sit down and rest a little while."

"Are we ready? Are all prompters at go?" Synthia was normally relaxed and at ease in front of the camera. She was obviously not herself this evening.

"It's okay, Synthia," said Anthony Sellers, the station's head cameraman. "All's well, as usual. You okay?"

"I'm sorry, Tony, too much coffee today."

"No problem, love. We are at four, three, two…"

"This is The People's View News Station Special Report with Synthia Godbold-Pearson. I am coming to you this evening with a special investigative segment that we have entitled New Passage Academy—The Inner-City Scandal.

"For the past few weeks there has been a multitude of protests and volatile commentary in response to this issue. Rumors have been all over the place as to the actual existence of a secret school that, with the parents' permission, teaches and raises the child. Be it editorials, blogs, or radio talk shows, there has been intense discussion regarding this story." She paused to gather herself as she turned and focused on a different camera. Her back was now straighter, her tone more crisp.

"All right, you go girl," whispered Anthony.

"As a professional rule, reporters must keep his or her individual opinion from entering any news story. We are admonished to maintain our objectivity by keeping our personal distance. In this regard, I have failed." Synthia again paused and willed her breathing to maintain its steadiness. She did not want the events of the past few days to come to her mind and alter what she considered to be the most important message to her viewers. Even though lives had been in jeopardy, the task at hand was to clearly convey the story and deliver her points. She continued her report.

"We at The People's View News Station have discovered that the rumors were not unfounded. That is, there does exist a secret preparatory academy. This academy has, for the past twenty-nine years, been educating and raising a select few children of inner-city communities of various cities. Philadelphia was one of them. It is also true that parents were essentially signing their children over to this covert institution." Synthia forced a slower verbal cadence as she added, "Young mothers were restricted to two to three visits per year with their young offspring." She allowed the last statement to sink into the psyche of her listening audience. "My dear listeners, this is where a good portion of this report does become somewhat personal. I ask that you indulge me for just a moment." She looked into the camera. "You see," she continued, "the argument of this school is the concept of the greater good. That is that the child will be so much better off being raised by New Passage Academy. Oh, I understand the argument. I know full well how some of our public school systems are failing our children. I also remember as a child how I was not only teased, but actually ridiculed, for wanting to excel academically." There was a perceptible decrease in the volume of Synthia's voice. Anthony believed that Synthia had lost her place or that something was wrong with the teleprompter. He immediately realized that an inner struggle was taking place within the heart of his favorite news anchor. His fingers tensed on the camera's controls. He relaxed when he heard the strong voice of Synthia come through the headset.

"I was chastised for wanting to be white," said Synthia. "The mindset of many of my peers was that to be an honor student, to actually entertain aspirations for schools of higher learning was to be in denial of my race! My God, how many of our students have accepted academic mediocrity and transformed the concept into a badge of honor? So I know why some people might lend an ear toward such a school as New Passage Academy. But, Philadelphians, also know that our investigation raised flags. Even though the cause may be noble, anything that rails against the basic tenets of motherhood, or that is borne in secret, is bound to breed problems. Secrets are close cousin to lies. Both tend to produce multiple and dark offspring. What we have unraveled in this investigation is that New Passage Academy hid some dark secrets. There were not many, but even so, it underscores the inherent problems in dealing with an unregulated entity no matter how benevolent the mission." Only a few could hear the whispered addendum to her last statement as she concluded with, "amen." Anthony offered a private smile having deciphered the religious reference. Synthia's posture and voice took on a more serious tone.

"I personally visited the academy and while profoundly impressed, I did come across a distressful situation that led to the unraveling of the presence of a woefully disintegrating administration. Philadelphia, many of you will be happy to know that the academy is no longer open. To their credit, however, they did not simply return the children to their respective homes. All of the children and their parents were giving the option of applying to other prestigious academic institutions, again at no cost to any family." Synthia turned to look toward camera number two. "So, ladies and gentlemen, the New Passage Academy has closed its doors. There will be no other family that will have to be presented with the agonizing decision of releasing their child to be raised by others." Her voice began to break. "Before we raise our glasses and bruise ourselves with repetitive pats on our backs, let's give this situation one more look." She held her gaze on the cameras.

"As I stated at the onset of this report, the title of this report is New Passage Academy, The Inner-City Scandal. I hold true to the title, ladies and gentlemen, but please allow me to clarify something." Synthia momentarily bit down on her lip so that the brief pain might hold back her emotions. "The Inner-City

Scandal has very little to do with the New Passage Academy. The Inner-City Scandal is specifically directed toward the perpetual acceptance of our public school system. When the rumors first surfaced, how many editorials talk shows, news reports, and radio arguments took place regarding New Passage Academy? Yet we have been numbingly accepting to a system whose graduation rate for an American city is... criminal. How dare we get angry and mobilize a call to arms, regarding the recruiting and philosophical practices of New Passage Academy, when so many are guilty of granting wholesale acceptance of our current, inner-city public school systems?

"The village rose and marched to the castle with their respective torches of protest: meanwhile we allowed other leaders to consistently render a profound disservice to our innocent children? In this high-tech society, why is it that the most recent technological acquisition by many public schools is not a computer or a laboratory, but a metal detector? Where's the same outcry when the basketball team can boast of a shiny new gym floor while the chess team has to meet in a leaky classroom that also serves as a storage center? Where's the debate? Where is the protest? With this failure of protest there remains no reason for the political powers that be to grant anything other than token, academic Band-Aids. These same politicians are understandably patient as they fully understand that most school protests and battle cries— while dramatic—shall certainly be brief." She switched cameras again.

"Swords were drawn as we lamented the hundreds of parents who chose not to actually raise their own children. Yet it's all right that during those thirty years or so, that thousands of children did not receive the best education that this rich country had to offer?

"It is no secret that our sincere, community leaders understand how the media can assist them in problem-solving. It is also no secret how a few will gladly trade their position on a topic for a visible position on the mayor's podium.

"Unfortunately, there are no boundaries that power worshipers cannot cross: even a few of our Sunday-morning leaders find room for compromise. The power of the camera's floodlights has successfully swayed more than one preacher's opinion, allowing political access to his or her pulpit. Of course, that minister now feels elevated among his religious peers. The quest for power is a human handicap, granting no exclusions."

Synthia placed her hands on the top of studio desk, clasping them together. She briefly looked toward the ceiling, debating her next comment. Anthony took his eyes away from his monitor. He needed to see Synthia's natural face. He could almost reach out from behind the camera and touch her passion. He quickly returned his eyes to his monitor as Synthia turned toward his camera to complete her report. "Why should a parent have to send their child to school, praying that the child wins the academic lottery and is assigned a capable and compassionate teacher—I salute them all—versus one whose primary concern is the countdown to retirement? Philadelphia, the true inner-city scandal is that this country has lowered the academic bar of our inner-city children, feeding all with a revised and deceptive level of intellectual expectation. The only reason that many have survived to date is because concerned and competent teachers take it upon themselves to go the extra mile to motivate and extract excellence from these precious young minds.

"This country and even many of its victims have numbed themselves into the perpetual acceptance of marginal performance. This vicious psychological cycle continues as good teachers lose their educational vigor and good students lose their aspirations. As this occurs the victims veer towards our nation's disheartening public school statistics, falsely perpetuating America's perception of teachers and students." She cleared her throat. "Before I close, I must end this report regarding the benefactors or financiers of New Passage Academy. The school was organized and maintained anonymously by a core of frustrated philanthropists. I initially believed that I had received the list of those persons and wanted to dramatically close this report by revealing those names to all. However, it has come to my attention that the names could not be authenticated. Therefore, I cannot put the station in a libelous position by reading out any non-confirmed names. The list was questionable. I have since destroyed it and will await receipt of a truly authenticated report." She smiled at the camera.

"As I conclude this special report, having probably satisfied many with the exposure of the New Passage Academy, I trust that a few will have found some understanding in what I have tried to convey. So rest easy. New Passage Academy will no longer be using the proverbial chalk on its classroom boards. I remind you, however, do not throw the chalk away. It may still be needed for the never-ending body outlines in the street. Where do we go from here? I await your answer. Good night."

CHAPTER **THIRTY-EIGHT**

Synthia nodded to the security officer as she stepped outside of the news building and drew in the evening air. She was properly rewarded with the scent of night breezes and exhaust fumes that were touched with a hint of rancid waste, an acquired taste. Her car was parked in her reserved spot, safe in the lower parking area of the building. After rendering her spirit-draining special report, she wanted to remain close to life. Her program had not only uncovered the workings of New Passage Academy, but it had also revealed a good portion of her soul. She did not want to immediately ease into the comfort and solace of her quiet vehicle. She wanted to see the city, to see faces and remind herself that she was a part of it all.

"Had a feeling that I'd be seeing you out here." The voice was low but piercing enough to break through the sounds of the active street. Synthia smiled. She stopped and gave a graceful turn toward a shimmering charcoal-gray limousine.

"Good evening, Mr. Franklin… or can I still call you Joseph?"

"I would be greatly disappointed if you did not," said a grinning Joseph Franklin. "What, did you think that I'd be angry? Please, let's ride awhile."

Synthia joined her friend in the limousine and gave a knowing nod to the driver.

"Here, let me pour you some chilled fruit juice," said Joseph. "It's good for the energy."

"Why yes, that would be nice. Thank you."

"So you thought your old friend was going to hold a grudge and all?" said Joseph.

"Oh no, not exactly. Come to think of it, I didn't really know how you'd take it."

Franklin waved a dismissive hand. "Please, Synthia, you have no cause for concern here. We all knew that this day would come. We really didn't expect for it to last this long. My colleagues and I actually believed that the problem with this whole public school system would have been fixed by now. Remember that this all started almost thirty years ago. Who knew that the problems could get worse?" Franklin exhaled as he bowed his head for a moment.

"I'm so sorry, Joseph, I know that you all meant well."

"No, my lady, I am fine. My heart is heavy not for the school but for the many who never received the opportunity for a full chance in life's journey." He reached over and clasped Synthia's hands. "I'm so proud to know you tonight. You see, like I said, we never expected it to last this long. We also never expected that our objective would be concluded with so much passion. We aren't perfect, Synthia. We tried to make a strong difference, but we became distracted and did not keep up our guard. As in many things, evil is always seeking a way in to disrupt and devour those things that are designed to be good and noble. Shame on us for not remembering that fundamental tenet; we should have been more watchful. We have walked for too long to have made such an error." He reached over to open the moon roof, allowing the night sky to enter the limousine. He gazed into the sky as if he were pleading for an answer to a private question.

With her hand still in his firm but gentle grasp, Synthia spoke: "Joseph, please, it wasn't your fault. You couldn't be everywhere." Franklin gave her a look that almost gave voice to a response. A response that would be contrary to her statement regarding one's ability to be omnipresent. He gave a small pause and leaned forward to pour more apricot juice. Synthia gratefully took the refreshing beverage and joined Franklin in watching the sky. "Yes, the night sky can be pretty."

Synthia thought it funny how she hadn't realized that at times, the city's sky still allowed a clear view of the celestial bodies. *I guess many things look different from the back seat of a high-end limousine.* For a while neither said a word, each seeking personal understanding amongst the distant stars. The moment was one of those rare times when an extended silence between two people was not awkward. Kindred spirits provided permission for them to be at ease in their late, evening musing.

Franklin finally broke the silence. "I need to thank you for what you did regarding the names of the benefactors. The list I forwarded to you was indeed quite accurate."

"Maybe it was, or maybe it wasn't. If I receive a list from someone who is used to holding secrets, should I not doubt its authenticity? How do you say it: consider the source?" Synthia leaned her head back further, closing her eyes after giving Franklin a wink.

"I guess they do say that sometimes."

Synthia lowered her voice. "Tell me, Joseph, would you do it again? You know, with all the stuff that has happened, all the pain that was caused. I'm not judging or anything, just curious." She did not rush him to answer.

"My dear Synthia, I have learned that to fear doing good just opens up a wider highway for evil. Good people and causes will always be around to stand in the gap. People may not be perfect, nor their methods of battle, but they must still press forward." He took a deep breath. "You see, Synthia, evil has the privilege of reckless abandonment. It doesn't have to weigh things out or even have a visible plan of action. It gleefully tries to touch and harm all in its way, knowing that man's own distrust will nurture its malice. Years ago, educational problems stemmed from a more overtly racist America. We were fighting America's longtime concept of inherent inferiority. Today the enemy appears to have creatively infiltrated our ranks. We now have to battle against a few soldiers from our own troops. These misled soldiers cannot even see that there remains a war. For some it's Friday night, and all is well. Let's party." He turned to Synthia. "You have a good and honest heart, Synthia, yet you were less than truthful regarding the list of names. I truly gave you a valid list. But you see, young lady, I also knew that the names were safe."

Synthia sat up and stared at Franklin "How do you know that I didn't make a copy? How did you know that I wouldn't divulge the names?"

"Perhaps you have made a copy, it's all right," said Franklin. "What I absolutely know is that you cannot turn away from who you are, Mrs. Godbold-Pearson. Others might, but not you. That's why I chose you."

"What you mean you chose me? I was contacted by an ex-school principal who put me on to the school. I would have found you on my own."

His warm eyes met Synthia's. "No, my dear. You may have eventually located the school, but unless I permit it, I cannot be found. As you may recall, it was this same car that beckoned you from outside that restaurant." She recalled their first meeting and gave a puzzled look toward Franklin. "Sorry, don't mean to keep being so confusing. It's just that I have long since understood that you possess a compassion and integrity not like most others."

"What you mean? Have you been watching me?"

"No, my dear, not in the sense of spying or stalking. You are, of course, a news anchor, and I was able to find your spirit simply by watching you." It wasn't that Synthia felt used or violated, but she did sense that her friend could do just what he said. *What did he mean when he said that no one could find him unless he allowed it?* Yet he existed in plain sight. She felt it best to change the subject.

"So you think that the boy will be all right? You know, the abducted one?"

Franklin closed his eyes before he answered. "It will certainly be a long struggle, but we'll see to it that the Sanford family's lives will be long, prosperous, and peaceful." Synthia started to ask Franklin just how he could be so confident regarding the future but held back her query. She didn't know why, but somehow she was certain that it would be so. The limousine once again fell into a peaceful silence. Synthia suddenly realized that she was beginning to nod off. She turned to speak to her silent friend but Franklin spoke first.

"The hour is getting late, Synthia. Allow me to drive you home. My car will pick you up tomorrow and take you to your car, or wherever you may wish to go. I'm sure that your husband would not wish for you to drive home when you are so tired." Synthia did not even bother with the usual courtesy reply of how it should be okay to drive herself home. Somehow she knew that the verbal ritual was not necessary, and truly, she believed it to be a good idea.

Franklin nudged his sleeping friend. "Ah, here we are my dear, safely home."

Home already? thought Synthia.

"Joseph, someday you and I will really have to sit down and have a serious conversation. You are indeed the most familiar stranger I know." She leaned over and gave him a small kiss on his cheek.

"Oh, what was that for?" He smiled.

"Just saying thank you for everything. By meeting you, I've gotten more questions than answers, but I've loved every minute of it. Also, I do thank you for what you and your associates tried to do with those children. I'm very sorry that a great school had to close down. It seems like there could have been some sort of compromise." Synthia got out of the car and leaned into the open window.

"Will you be keeping in touch, or will my special friend be fading into the background?"

"I'm always around, my daughter. I'll always be near but it's probably time for me to pay more attention to other ventures. This episode has also taught me much. Don't you ever feel guilty, Synthia. You've performed a good service. Don't ever feel bad about the closing of New Passage Academy East, okay?"

"Okay, Joseph. Take care of yourself, and look in on me whenever you get a chance."

"Count on it." He winked as the limousine eased into the flow of the city traffic.

Walking into the gleaming entranceway, Synthia greeted her doorman. Although her body was weary, her steps enjoyed a childlike spring as she strolled toward the elevator. She reached the elevator and placed her finger on the up button. Her finger stayed there. The doorman glanced back to ensure the safety of his female charge, wondering if all was well.

Synthia's hand slid down to her side, remaining rigid, still pointing. The elevator had answered the electronic summons and opened its decorative doors. The doors soon closed, still without a passenger. Synthia gave a slow turn toward the lobby door, her face finally releasing its subconscious tension. The words came forth slowly and firmly: "New Passage Academy *East*?"

CHAPTER THIRTY-NINE

Sweet wafts of cinnamon and freshly ground coffee billowed in from the kitchen and into the large bedroom of Chadric and Synthia. Synthia hugged her satin pillow for a moment as the pleasant struggle of sleep versus breakfast played out its usual morning rivalry. This morning hunger and warm aromas gave sleep little ammunition; it bid farewell to its now awakened host.

"Good morning, sleepyhead," said Chadric as he set down the wooden breakfast table in front of his smiling wife.

"Mmm, good morning to you. I can tell that someone has been busy in the kitchen."

"Just making a little pick-me-up breakfast for my wife, the crusader."

"Oh hush Chadric, and get in bed so we can nibble down these scrumptious-looking, cinnamon pancakes."

"Why thank you. For a moment there I thought that you were going to keep it all for yourself." Chadric removed his slippers and slipped into the bed next to Synthia.

"The coffee is great, honey. It's nice and bold today, something new?"

"No, nothing new, just a little more of it. You came in late last night, seemed a little bushed, so I thought that I would give you a little extra morning caffeine boost."

"Yes, I do need it, love. What do you say that after breakfast we take a morning ride and go pick up my car at the news station?"

"Is everything all right with your car, or did you just have your boyfriend drop you off last night?"

She laughed. "No. The car is fine, and I told my boyfriend that I had to get home a little earlier last night."

"Don't tell me our Mr. Joseph Franklin, right?"

"Yes. We had a little talk after my special news program last night. That man continues to baffle me."

"Yes, he's always been that way. I imagine."

Synthia slowly chewed on a bite of pancake. She kept her head down as she softly posed a question to her husband.

"Chadric, I know that we agreed that we would not talk about it, but do you regret your time at New Passage Academy?"

Chadric paused to fix the pillows behind his head. "You know, sweetie, in spite of everything, I don't regret it." He reached one hand and found Synthia's. "Somehow I don't feel that I would have had the opportunity to meet and marry Ms. Synthia Godbold. I'm not talking about any financial security that we enjoy. I'm simply speaking about the capacity to simply enjoy. Let's not speak about the past." He stroked her arm. "New Passage Academy has shuttered its windows. Good or bad, its time has passed and communities have to find their own way in this fight for education. I'm just thankful that I can sit in a large king-size bed on a lazy Saturday morning and eat pancakes naked with my loving wife. So let's just say that school is out."

"But we're not naked, dear."

"Can you for once just go with the story? Now, didn't it sound better? But no, my wife just has to—" He caught a pillow full flush in the face. He smiled and removed his temporary facial mask and placed it behind his head. He turned toward Synthia with an apologetic pout.

"What say we pick up the car later this afternoon? We'll just be lazy and watch some old cowboy movies in bed."

"Sounds lovely, darling; we might even get naked."

"Hey!" Synthia clicked on the TV and found the Nostalgic Channel.

"Oh, there's one," said Chadric, "Go West Young Man. Now that's an old one. This one is with Mae West and Randolph Scott. Man, it must have been exciting to establish new frontiers in the West eh, sweetie? I guess everybody couldn't stay in the east." Synthia did not respond. She was once again lost in thought. Go west? She sat her orange juice down and turned toward the window. A small but knowing smile came to her face as she softly whispered, "I guess those early pioneers did what they truly believed needed to be done." She gave her husband a delicate kiss on his lips. "Yes, Chadric, honey, I guess they did."

CHAPTER FORTY

The campus of Peabody University was a hallmark display of burnt-orange and crimson leaves that shimmered in the late October wind. Nora Sanford left her two-bedroom apartment, making her way to her 8:15am Childhood Studies class. She passed many young faces along the way; some nodded in recognition while others remained attached to their electronic body appendages. She was feeling good. She had been up half the night studying for her exam. She dared not disappoint her patient professor by achieving anything less than a 'B' on her paper. Part of the difficulty in studying was the fact that Nora still could not believe that she was a college student. Here she was— seventeen years after high school graduation, a freshman. She loved it!

The educational miracle had occurred soon after LeDain's return home. For days LeDain had clung to his mother, imploring her to never leave him again. Twice a week he was seeing a counselor that had been provided by the academy. Thankfully, he was showing rapid progress in dealing with the events of the past six months. Nora was initially worried about LeDain's return to the public school system. She was concerned that he would have great difficultly in adapting to a less disciplined atmosphere. She was relieved when she was made aware of the fact that all the students of New Passage Academy would have fully paid options regarding admittance to other traditional private schools. Still, it would be of no value if LeDain did not want to be away from his mother, and nor did she want him to go.

Months ago, to Nora's surprise, she received a visit from an elderly lawyer, Leonard Ogden. Mr. Ogden had informed her that not only had New Passage Academy found an excellent school for LeDain, but that Nora would be going along with him. Nora reminded the lawyer of her financial status. Unfortunately, relocation was out of the question for her; she and LeDain would have to make it where they were.

"Please, Mrs. Sanford, allow me to be very clear on this proposal," said Mr. Ogden. "If he so desires, LeDain has fully paid admission to Baptiste-Darwin Preparatory Academy. It is a school located in Virginia. As a matter of fact, it is not far from Peabody University."

"I think that I've heard of Peabody University," said Nora. "But—"

The lawyer quickly interrupted her. "I'm glad that you've heard of the university, Mrs. Sanford, because that is where you have been enrolled." The pause in the air was long.

Unknowingly, Nora began to stutter. "Wha…what do you mean that, that I've been enrolled?" said Nora. "I'm not college material!"

Although a stranger, the elderly lawyer fixed a grandfatherly look at the astonished woman.

"I think that you will excuse us if we beg to differ, Mrs. Sanford. Who gave you permission to deny your capabilities? I know that Mrs. Matthews certainly did not." Nora's hands held on to the armrest of the chair, unsuccessful in her attempt to control her shaking. Her eyes found Mr. Ogden's.

"Mrs. Sanford, we do not desire to separate you from your son. We have already secured a two-bedroom apartment for you and LeDain. The rent and all the utilities will be paid by my clients for a period of five years. During those years you will have an educational stipend in the amount of $2,000 a month. That amount is to cover all other household needs and incidentals that you and LeDain may require. Mrs. Sanford, all this is done with the expectation that you satisfy the preliminary requirements and then enroll as a full-time student at Peabody University. Your major is totally up to you; although, Mrs. Matthews believes that you would be an excellent elementary school teacher. By the way, she asked me to tell you that this is an easy riddle to solve." Nora was trembling. She could barely move as her guest stood to bid her goodbye.

Leonard Ogden walked over and stood in front of Nora. "Truly, it has been my honor and pleasure to present this to you today. It is not often that I receive such a noble assignment. Please forgive me for the intrusion and also for this." He leaned over and gave Nora a kiss on the cheek. Nora looked up and blushed, smiling. "I fully understand that that was not a traditional or legal vehicle for closing the deal," said Mr. Ogden. "But it just felt appropriate. I do hope that the name Nora Sanford is on the freshman list this fall. It would be my honor to one day receive an invitation to a baccalaureate ceremony for one Mrs. Nora Ellise Sanford."

Mr. Ogden adjusted his bow tie and left Nora stunned, still rooted to her chair. As he closed the door behind him, he could hear her crying. Nora had fell to her knees, prostrate in her emotional release. He paused and slightly turned his head toward the door and smiled. Leonard Ogden smoothed the front of his suit and turned toward his automobile. The blurriness of his wet eyes caused a brief delay in making it to his car. He didn't mind. You better watch yourself, he thought. Somebody's gonna think that lawyers are actually human. He laughed at his thoughts as he took one last look at the home of Nora Sanford. "Bless you, bless you both."

CHAPTER **FORTY-ONE**

The steps of the stout stranger were noticeably slower. His back formed an uncomfortable, anatomical question mark. He walked into the emergency room. He had been careful to empty his pockets of anything that would prove to be curious to strange eyes. The .38 revolver had been left at the police station. *No questions asked* remained the order of the day so no words had been spoken to the curious officer. Besides, the stranger realized that he no longer required the gun. His loved ones were no longer in any danger. He patiently waited his turn: he was used to being in lines. Time didn't seem to matter anymore.

"Rich or poor, no man gets any less," he used to remark to anyone who would listen. A hospital emergency room was just another line, a perverse line of the clinically challenged. When his name was finally called, it took a few moments for the stranger to rise from his gum-encrusted seat. Despite his discomfort, he managed a gentleman's nod to the young woman who guided him to a gurney in the corner of the crowded emergency area. He again smiled as the young aide gave him instructions to remove his clothing. The stranger was told that someone would be right with him. A smile came even though he knew that no one was likely to be right with him, that he had merely graduated into another line. He was growing tired. He closed his eyes and he drifted off to sleep.

"Hello, Mr. Smith. Can you hear me?" The voice came from the leader of a group of physicians who were gathered around the front of the stranger's bed. The stranger realized that the doctor must have repeated the name several times. The problem was that Smith was not his real name and therefore the man had failed to immediately recognize that he was being addressed. The difficulty in focusing was also caused by the many IV lines and various tubes that sought to entangle him. He sensed a funny, plastic smell then realized that an oxygen mask was strapped to his face.

Hell, I felt more comfortable last week, he thought. He then tried to remember how long he had been in the hospital. He wasn't sure. The doctor spoke again.

"My name is Doctor Shuttleford and these are my associates." He glanced at the other fresh-faced physicians. *Yeah, associates, right,* thought Mr. Smith. He forced a weak smile at the entourage of medical students.

"Mr. Smith, it seems that your heart has suffered a great bit of damage, seems that it has been that way for a while. We've been testing you for the last four days, and to be quite frank, we don't like what we see. Mr. Smith, it appears that you have sustained significant and long-term damage to your heart. In certain situations you would probably be a candidate for a transplant but other medical factors may make that difficult."

Oh, I guess now we're going to bring up my little liver problem, thought Mr. Smith. Wasn't even my fault. I was never a drinker or nothing, just got caught up with the wrong doctor prescribing me some half-studied medications that almost killed me. Hmm, I guess it will finish the job now.

The doctor moved closer. "What we plan to do is to make sure that you remain as comfortable as possible."

"What do you mean as comfortable as possible?" said Mr. Smith. At least that's what he tried to say. His voice, once strong, now escaped as a coarse whisper. *What goes here?* he thought. He tried again to speak and finally found his voice.

"Just what do you plan to do doctor?" This time the words came a little clearer, yet his voice remained weak and foreign.

"First of all, Mr. Smith, let me ask you; do you have any relatives near by? It's just that we have not been able to track anyone down. How about any real close friends?" Mr. Smith took another deep breath, though it still didn't seem to satisfy his body's oxygen need, and gazed toward the ceiling lights. For a moment he observed the flickering of a struggling bulb.

"No, there is no one, doctor. My family is gone. They were beautiful once, but no more family. It's okay, doctor. No need to check for anybody, I'm fine."

A few days later, Michelle, the night nurse entered Mr. Smith's room. His heart monitor had revealed multiple arrhythmias throughout the day. It was almost 2:30 in the morning. She wanted to peek in on her ill patient. Two days ago Mr. Smith had informed the doctors that he wanted no heroic measures on his behalf and that he was content in whatever lay before him. For some reason, although very busy, Dr. Shuttleford had spent a little more time with Mr. Smith. It was not because of any prolonged questioning by his patient, but the fact that he had never witnessed such composure from any of his terminal patients. Mr. Smith's acceptance was not based in defeat or surrender to death but of the acceptance of life. He whispered to his physician that although his life was filled with many mistakes and regrets, he understood that those were all a part of his particular life.

"There is no such thing as a perfect walk, Dr. Shuttleford. I still got some burdens that I don't know what to do with, but I understand that they were for me to carry. Some I learned to set down, but no man walks free."

Michelle walked to his bedside. She could tell that Mr. Smith's breathing had become more labored. She glanced at his IV to confirm that all was well and that his sedation was being properly administered. A quick downward glance informed Michelle that Mr. Smith was looking back at her. She leaned down to inquire if he was all right or in needed of anything. His breathing mimicked the sound of a baby's gurgle; she realized that he was trying to say something.

"Can I get you anything, Mr. Smith?" she said. The words escaped as if coming through the end of a rolled piece of cardboard.

"I guess there's nothing more for me to get, young lady. I do want to thank you for being kind to a stranger."

"But you're my patient, Mr. Smith."

He managed a half-smile. "I know, but I also know that people knows a nobody when they sees one. But you were still kind." He grimaced as he struggled to continue.

"Don't try to talk right now, Mr. Smith," said Michelle. "You just rest and we will talk tomorrow."

"No. No more tomorrows. This body's done had a long yesterday." His voice lowered even more as the words desired to rest in his throat, to not make the final voyage through his mouth. "Wasn't perfect, but always did try to do right by my family."

"Is there some family that you wish for me to call?"

"No family. But I did try to do right by them. I'm still ashamed of what I did, what I felt I had to do. Had to walk away from my child, loved him though. Just tried to protect my family, always try to protect my family: my child." He spoke no more. Michelle didn't even realize that she was holding his hand until she felt her tears lightly splash on their clasped union. She remained there for a moment. Mr. Smith had officially desired no heroic efforts and therefore there was no need to summon help to his room.

"Yes, Mr. Smith, you had a long yesterday. You rest now and I pray that God will grant you blessed tomorrows." As Michelle slowly released his grip, she noticed a small, faded picture partially wedged under Mr. Smith's side. It was that of a little boy. She turned on the overhead light to get a better look at the worn and cracked photograph. It was a school picture. The child looked like he might have been in first grade. *What a beautiful child,* she thought. She again looked at the still form of her deceased patient.

"I believe that you did have family, Mr. Smith, and such a handsome looking boy. I believe that you did have some wonderful yesterdays." She turned the picture over to see if any other information might be there. The year had been smeared away but Michelle could make out the smudged name: *Chadric.*

INDENTURED SCHOLARS:
The Inner City Scandal

by W. Ivan Wright

INDENTURED
SCHOLARS
the inner city scandal

ABOUT THE AUTHOR

W. Ivan Wright is a native of Trenton, New Jersey where he attended the city's public school system. He is a graduate of Indiana University of Pennsylvania and holds a B. S. in Respiratory Therapy.

Ivan's first book, **Black People: For Entertainment Purposes Only** is a suspense thriller that speaks to the awesome power of perception.

Mature characters and themes in Ivan's books candidly and humorously allow the reader to peer at the cultural intricacies that express the African American experience.

W. Ivan Wright is passionate about expanding the visual horizons of our young people. He is available for public events and speaking engagements.

Please contact: ivanwright.com